HARLEQ...

GRAYSON

USA TODAY BESTSELLING AUTHOR
DELORES FOSSEN

Recycling programs for this product may not exist in your area.

ISBN-13: 978-1-335-40573-9

Grayson
First published in 2011. This edition published in 2021.
Copyright © 2011 by Delores Fossen

This edition published by arrangement with Harlequin Books S.A.

For questions and comments about the quality of this book, please contact us at CustomerService@Harlequin.com.

Harlequin Enterprises ULC
22 Adelaide St. West, 40th Floor
Toronto, Ontario M5H 4E3, Canada
www.Harlequin.com

Printed in U.S.A.

USA TODAY bestselling author **Delores Fossen** has sold over seventy novels with millions of copies of her books in print worldwide. She's received the Booksellers' Best Award, the *RT Book Reviews* Reviewers' Choice Award, and was a finalist for the prestigious RITA® Award. In addition, she's had nearly a hundred short stories and articles published in national magazines. You can contact the author through her webpage at www.deloresfossen.com.

Chapter 1

Silver Creek, Texas

Sheriff Grayson Ryland couldn't shake the feeling that someone was watching him.

He slid his hand over the Smith & Wesson in his leather shoulder holster and stepped from his patrol truck. He lifted his head, listening, and glanced around the thick woods that were practically smothering the yellow cottage. The front door and curtains were closed.

No sign of the cottage's owner, Eve Warren.

No sign of anyone for that matter, but just twenty minutes earlier Eve had called his office to report that she had seen someone *suspicious* in the area.

Grayson knew this part of the county like the back of his hand. Along with his brothers, he had fished in the creek at the bottom of the hill. He'd camped these woods. There were a lot of places to duck out of sight....

Plenty of memories, too.

That required a deep breath, and he cursed himself for having to take it.

The front door opened, and he spotted Eve. She was a five-foot-six-inch memory of a different kind. She'd obviously known he was there. Maybe that was the reason his brain was firing warnings on all cylinders.

"Grayson," she said, her tongue flickering over her bottom lip. "You came."

That nervous little tongue flicker and the too-hopeful look in her misty blue eyes riled him. "You called the sheriff's office and asked for me," he reminded her. "You said you thought you saw someone."

"Of course." She nodded, swallowed hard. "But I wasn't sure you'd come."

Neither was he, especially since he was neck-deep in a murder investigation, but when he'd gotten her message, he'd decided not to send a deputy, that he would be the one to personally respond.

Well, respond to the call anyway.

Not to the woman.

Not ever again.

It'd been over sixteen years since he'd last seen Eve. She'd been standing in a doorway then, too. Her blond hair had been well past her shoulders back in those days, but it was short now and fashionably rumpled. The last decade and a half had settled nicely on her curvy body.

Something he decided not to notice.

Since his eyes and body seemed to have a different idea about that not-noticing part, Grayson got down to business.

"You reported someone suspicious?" he prompted.

"I did." She scrubbed her hands down the sides of her pearl-gray dress. The cold December wind caught the hem, making it flutter around the tops of her knees. "I was about to call you anyway…about something else… and then I saw him. A man. He was down by the creek."

Grayson lifted his shoulder and wondered why the heck she'd intended to call him, but he didn't ask. "Could have been a neighbor." Even though there weren't any close ones to the Warren cottage.

"I don't think it was a neighbor," Eve insisted. "I got a bad feeling when I spotted him."

Yeah. Grayson knew all about bad feelings. The one he had about this situation was getting worse with each passing moment.

"I didn't want to take any chances," she continued. "What with the murder you had here a few days ago. How are you handling that, by the way?"

She probably hadn't meant to irritate him with that question, but she did. Hell, no matter what she said, she would irritate him. But Grayson didn't want anyone, including Eve, questioning his ability to handle a murder investigation, even if it was only the third one in his twelve years as sheriff of Silver Creek.

"I heard you haven't identified the body, or the killer," she added.

"Not yet." And Grayson got back on target. "You have any idea who this person was you saw?"

Eve shook her head. "No. But for the past couple of days I've been getting hang-up calls at my condo in San Antonio. And there's been a time or two when I thought someone was following me. Nothing specific. Just a feeling. It was one of the reasons I decided to come out to the cottage. So I could get away."

Well, that explained that. Eve had inherited the cottage from her grandmother eighteen months ago, but to the best of Grayson's knowledge, this was her first visit to the place. And she hadn't just come to relax. She'd planned on calling him.

Why?

Again, he didn't ask. He kept this conversation focused on the job he'd been called out to do.

"Any reason you know of why someone would follow you or make those hang-up calls?" he asked.

Another head shake. "I've been under a lot of stress lately," she admitted. "The job. And some personal stuff. Until I saw the man, I kept telling myself that it was all in my head. But he was real, Grayson."

He mentally groaned at the way she said his name. It was intimate, the way she used to murmur it after one of their scalding hot kissing sessions.

He glanced at the woods, then the creek. "I'll have a look around," Grayson let her know. "But if you're worried, you probably shouldn't be staying out here alone."

He turned to have that look around.

"Wait," Eve called out. "Don't go. I wanted to ask about your family. How are your brothers?"

He had four living brothers. Four sets of news, updates and troubles. Since it would take the better part of an hour to catch her up on everything, Grayson settled for saying, "They're all fine."

Grayson turned again, but again Eve stopped him.

"Even Nate?" she questioned. "I heard his wife was killed a few months ago."

Yeah. That was all part of the troubles. The worst of them. "Nate's coping." But Grayson knew that wasn't true. If Nate didn't have his baby daughter to care for, his brother wouldn't make it out of bed each morning. Grayson was still trying to figure out how to take care of that.

"And the ranch?" Eve continued. "I read somewhere that the ranch won a big award for your quarter horses."

Fed up with the small talk, Grayson decided to put an end to this. Chitchat was an insult at this stage of the game. However, when he looked back at her, he saw that she had her hands clenched around the door frame. Her knuckles were turning white.

Grayson cursed under his breath. "Okay. What's wrong?" But he didn't just ask. He went closer so he could see inside the cottage to make sure someone wasn't standing behind her, holding her at gunpoint. Because

Eve wasn't the white-knuckle type. He had never known anything to scare her.

The place was small so he was able to take in most of it with one sweeping glance. There was no one in the living and eating area, and the loft/bedroom was empty, too.

Grayson looked her straight in the eyes. "Eve, are you all right?"

She hesitated and nibbled some more on her lip. "I really did see someone about a half hour ago, I swear, and he ran away when he spotted me."

Since that sounded like the beginning of an explanation that might clarify the real reason for her call, Grayson just stood there and waited for the rest of it.

"Could you come in?" Eve finally said. "I need to talk to you."

Oh, hell. This couldn't be good. "Talk?" he challenged.

He was about to remind her that it was long over between them, that they had no past issues to discuss, but she kept motioning for him to come in.

"Eve," he warned.

"Please." Her voice was all breath and no sound.

Grayson cursed that *please* and the look in her eyes. He knew that look. He'd seen it when she was thirteen and had learned her mother was dying from bone cancer. He'd seen it again sixteen years ago when on her twenty-first birthday she'd stood in the doorway of the ranch and demanded a commitment from him or else.

Because he'd had no choice, Grayson had answered *or else*.

And Eve had walked out.

Now, Grayson walked in. She stepped back so he could enter the cottage, and she shut the door behind him. He didn't take off his Stetson or his jacket because he hoped he wouldn't be here that long.

It was warm inside, thanks to the electric heater she had going near the fireplace. No fire, though. And it would have been a perfect day for it since the outside temp was barely forty degrees.

With a closer look, Grayson could see the place was in perfect order. Definitely no signs of any kind of struggle or hostage situation. There was no suitcase that he could spot, but Eve's purse was on the coffee table, and her camera and equipment bag were on the small kitchen counter. Several photographs were spread out around the bag. Since Eve was a newspaper photographer, that wasn't out of the ordinary, either.

"The pictures," she mumbled following his gaze. "I was trying to work while I waited for you."

Trying. And likely failing from the way they were scattered around. "Are you in some kind of trouble?"

"Yes," she readily admitted.

Surprised, and more worried than he wanted to be, he turned around to face her. "Trouble with the law?"

"I wish," Eve mumbled. She groaned softly and threaded her fingers through both sides of her hair. That stretched her dress over her breasts and gave Grayson a reminder he didn't want or need.

He'd been attracted to Eve for as long as he could remember. But he refused to let that attraction play into whatever the hell this was.

"Trouble at work?" he tried next.

She lifted her shoulder but answered, "No."

He glanced at the photos on the table again.

"I took those at a charity fund-raising rodeo in San Antonio," she explained.

So, they were work, but judging from the casual way she'd mentioned them, they weren't the source of the worry in her eyes. "Look, I could play twenty questions and ask about a stalker, an ex or whatever. But let's save ourselves some time and you just tell me what you have to say."

She nodded, paused, nodded again. "It's personal. And it has to do with you. I need to ask you something."

Grayson braced himself for some kind of rehashing of the past. After all, he was thirty-eight now, and Eve was thirty-seven. Hardly kids. And since neither of them had ever married, maybe this was her trip back down memory lane.

Well, he didn't want to take this trip with her.

"I've been having some medical problems," she continued. But then paused again.

That latest pause caused Grayson to come up with some pretty bad conclusions. Conclusions he didn't want to say aloud, but his first thought was cancer or some other terminal disease. Hell.

Had Eve come home to die?

"What's wrong?" he settled for repeating.

She shook her head, maybe after seeing the alarm in his eyes. "No. Not that kind of medical problem."

Grayson silently released the breath he'd been holding.

"I'm, uh, going through, well, menopause," she volunteered.

Of all the things Grayson had expected her to say, that wasn't one of them. "Aren't you too young for that?"

"Yes. Premature menopause." She swallowed hard again. "There's no way to stop it."

Well, it wasn't a cancer death sentence like her mother's, but Grayson could understand her concern. "So, is that why you're here, to try to come to terms with it?"

He'd asked the question in earnest, but he checked his watch. Talking with him wouldn't help Eve come to terms with anything, and he had work to do. That included a look around the place and then he had to convince her to head back to San Antonio. It was obvious she was too spooked and worried to be out in the woods all alone.

"I don't have much time," she said before he could speak. "That's why I came to Silver Creek today. And that's why I'll need your answer right away. I know this isn't fair, but if you say no, I'll have to try to find someone else…though I'm not sure I can." She didn't stop long enough to draw breath, and her words bled together. "Still, I'll understand if you want to say no, but Grayson, I'm praying you won't—"

"What are you talking about?" he finally said, speaking right over her.

Now Eve stopped and caught on to the back of the chair. "Perhaps you should sit down for this."

The rushed frantic pace was gone, but her eyes told him this particular storm was far from being over.

"I'd rather stand," he let her know.

"No. Trust me on this. You need to be sitting."

That took him several steps beyond just being curious, and Grayson sank into the chair across from her. Eve sat as well, facing him. Staring at him. And nibbling on her lip.

"I'm not sure how to say this," she continued, "so I'm just going to put it out there."

But she still didn't do that. Eve opened her mouth, closed it and stared at him.

"Grayson," she finally said and looked him straight in the eyes. "I need you to get me pregnant. *Today.*"

Chapter 2

Eve had tried to brace herself for Grayson's reaction.

She'd anticipated that he might just walk out. Or curse. Or even ask her if she'd lost her mind. He might still do those things, but at the moment he just sat there while his jaw practically hit his knees.

Other than his slack-jaw reaction, there was no sign of the storm that she must have stirred up inside him. Not that Eve had expected him to show any major signs of what he was feeling.

Grayson was Grayson.

Calm, reliable, levelheaded, responsible.

Hot.

In those well-worn Wranglers, black Stetson, black shirt and buckskin jacket, he looked like a model for some Western ad in a glossy magazine.

A comparison he would have hated if he had known what she was thinking.

Even though he had that scarred silver badge clipped to his rawhide rodeo belt, Grayson was first and foremost a cowboy and, along with his brothers, owner of one of the most successful ranches in central Texas. That success was due in large part to Grayson.

There was nothing glossy about him.

Eve forced herself away from that mental summary of Grayson's attributes. His hot cowboy looks and ranching success weren't relevant here. It had been the calm, reliable, levelheaded and responsible aspects of his personality that had caused her to want him to father her child.

Maybe it was her desperation, but Eve had hoped that Grayson would also be cooperative. That slack jaw gave her some doubts about that though.

"When I was at my doctor's office this morning, I found out I'm ovulating," she continued. That seemed way too personal to be sharing with anyone except maybe a spouse or best friend, but she didn't have time for modesty here.

Time was literally ticking away.

"The fact that I'm ovulating is nothing short of a miracle," she continued. "The doctor didn't think it would happen, and it almost certainly won't happen again."

Grayson just kept staring.

She wished he would curse or yell, but no, not Grayson. Those silver-gray eyes drilled right into her, challenging her to give him an explanation that he could wrap his logical mind around.

There wouldn't be anything logical about this. Well, not on his part anyway. To Eve, it was pure logic.

"I desperately want a child, and I'm begging you to help me," she clarified in case the gist had gotten lost in all her babbling. "I don't have time to find anyone else. I've got twenty-four hours, maybe less."

Grayson dropped the stare, blew out a long breath and leaned back in the chair. He was probably glad that she had insisted on the being seated part.

He flexed his eyebrows. "How can you possibly ask me to do this?"

"You're the first person I thought of," she admitted.

Actually, he was the *only* person. Those Ryland genes were prime stuff, and all the Ryland males were able-bodied, smart as whips and drop-dead gorgeous with their midnight-black hair and crystal-gray eyes. Again, the looks were just icing.

Grayson wasn't just her first choice for this. He was her *only* choice.

"Don't say no," Eve blurted out when she was certain Grayson was about to do exactly that.

Now he cursed. This time it wasn't under his breath. "No," he stated simply, but it had not been simply said. There was a flash of emotion in all those swirls of gray in his eyes. "You already know I don't want to be a father."

It was an argument that Eve had anticipated, and she had a counterargument for it. "Yes, because you had to raise your younger brothers after your father walked out and your mother died."

Now *she* cursed. She should have rehearsed this. Bringing up Grayson's reckless father was not the way to earn points here even though it'd happened over twenty years ago when Grayson was barely eighteen. A lifetime wouldn't be long enough to forget or forgive that kind of hurt, and it had shaped Grayson to the very core of who he was now.

Yes, he'd been a father figure to his five younger siblings. Head of the ranch and the family. And he'd sacrificed so much for both that by the time Eve had been looking to settle down and have a family with him, Grayson no longer had anything to give anyone.

Including her.

Still, she wanted him for this massive favor.

"I'm not asking you to be a father." Eve tried and failed to keep the emotion out of her argument, but her voice broke. "I only need you to get me pregnant, Grayson. Nothing else. In fact, I would insist on nothing else."

She hated to put him into a corner as she'd done all those years ago. That had been a massive mistake. But she did need an immediate answer.

Grayson shook his head again and eased to the edge of the chair so they were closer. And eye to eye.

"I can't." He held up his hand when she started to interrupt him. "I know the difference between fathering a child and being a father. I can't say yes to either."

Oh, mercy. He wasn't even giving it any thought or consideration. He had doled out an automatic refusal. Eve had thought she had prepared herself for this, but she obviously hadn't. That sent her desperation to a whole new level. Everything inside her started to race and spin as if she were on the verge of a panic attack.

She immediately tried to come up with other ways she could persuade him. First and foremost, she could try to use their past. Their connection. They'd been close once. Once, they'd been in love.

Well, she had been in love with him anyway.

Grayson never quite let himself take that leap of the heart, and he'd certainly never said the words.

She had hoped the close-to-love feelings that he had once had for her would be a trump card she could use here to convince him. Heck, she wasn't too proud to beg.

But she shook her head.

Begging might work. *Might.* However, this was Grayson, and because in the past she had loved him, Eve owed him more than that. She reined in her feelings and tried to say something that made sense. Something that would make him see that she wasn't crazy, just desperate.

"I'm sorry," she somehow managed to say. Her breath suddenly felt too thick to push out of her lungs, and she understood that whole cliché about having a heavy heart. Hers weighed a ton right now. "When the doctor told me I was ovulating and that I probably had a day or two at most, I thought of you. I jumped right in my car and drove straight to Silver Creek."

"I'm flattered. I think." The corner of his mouth lifted a fraction.

Ah, there it was. The biggest weapon in the Grayson Ryland arsenal. That half smile. Even now, after his refusal, it made her feel all warm and golden inside.

Since he'd attempted some levity, Eve did, too, but she doubted the smile made it to her eyes. God, this hurt. She wanted this baby more than her own life, and it was slipping away as the seconds ticked off.

"You can find someone else?" Grayson asked.

"I hope." But that was being overly optimistic. She'd lost a lot of time by driving out to Silver Creek, but then she'd had no choice. She very well couldn't have explained this with a phone call. Plus, she had prayed that she would be able to convince him once they were face-to-face.

She'd obviously been wrong.

Eve felt the raw blush on her cheeks and got to her feet. "I need to hurry back into San Antonio."

Grayson stood, as well. "Maybe you can use a sperm bank or fertility clinic?"

"No." She tried to blink back the tears, but failed at that, too. "Not enough time. The doctor said it takes days, even weeks to go through the screening and get an appointment. Plus, many of the clinics are closed because Christmas is only three days away."

He acknowledged that with a shrug. "A friend then?"

The drive had given her time to consider that, as well. It was sad but true that she was seriously lacking male companionship. Heck, she hadn't had a real date in nearly a year, and her last boyfriend was married now. As for male friends and coworkers, none had fit the bill as well as Grayson Ryland.

She shook her head and hurried to the kitchen where she crammed the photos back into her bag. The pictures were yet another kettle of fish, but they would have to wait. Eve wasn't ready to give up her baby mission just yet, even if she'd failed with Grayson.

She put on her red wool coat and hoisted both her purse and equipment bag onto her shoulder. Moving as fast as she could, she shut off the heater, unplugged it and turned back around to face Grayson. Even after his refusal, she couldn't help feeling that jolt of attraction when she looked at him.

Drop-dead gorgeous was right.

And for several brief moments Eve considered tossing the little bit of pride she had left. She could just throw herself at him and try to seduce him.

But she rethought that.

Grayson would resist. He had already shown her that he had a mountain of willpower and discipline to go along with those looks.

"What will you do?" he asked.

Because she felt the tears start to burn in her eyes, Eve dodged his gaze and grabbed her keys. "Maybe I can hire a friend of a friend."

She could make some calls the second she was back in her car, but she had no idea where to start.

"Hire someone?" Grayson questioned. He stepped outside the cottage with her.

Eve nodded. She closed and locked the door before she headed for her car. It wasn't below freezing, but the icy wind sliced right through her.

"You'd hire someone?" Grayson repeated when she didn't answer. He caught on to her arm and whirled her around to face him. "Eve, listen to yourself. Yes, I know you're desperate, and this baby must be important to you or you wouldn't have come here, but you can't just hire someone to sleep with you."

"To provide semen so I can be inseminated," she corrected, maneuvering herself out of his grip. She couldn't look at him and didn't want him to look at her. Eve hurried across the yard. "I have no intentions of sleeping with anyone to get pregnant. I was serious about not having a biological father in the picture. I'll make some calls, find a donor, pay him for his sperm and, if necessary, I'll do the insemination at home."

Grayson made a sound of relief, or something. Probably because he'd thought she was indeed crazy enough to jump into bed with the first guy she ran across on the drive home. Eve's biological clock was screaming for her to do that, but she wanted a healthy baby and body.

"I want to raise a baby on my own," she continued. "And if I find someone, he'll have to agree to giving up his paternal rights."

No need to rehash the emotional baggage that had brought her to that conclusion. Besides, Grayson knew about her absentee father and the abusive stepfather that she'd had as a kid. He didn't know about the three failed relationships she'd had since leaving Silver Creek, and that included one episode of her being an honest-to-goodness runaway bride.

It was just as well he didn't know that.

Best not to spell it out that she considered Grayson and only Grayson for a life partner. He was literally the only man she trusted, even if he had crushed her heart all those years ago. And now he'd managed to do it again.

Frustrated with herself and her situation, Eve threw open the back door of her car so she could dump her bag and equipment onto the seat. She hesitated for just a moment because she knew Grayson was right behind her. If she turned around, she'd have to face him once more.

"I'm sorry I bothered you," Eve mumbled.

She turned and, still dodging his gaze, she tried to sidestep around Grayson.

He sidestepped, too, and blocked her path. She hadn't thought it possible, but he looked more uncomfortable than she felt.

"I can call the Silver Creek Hospital," Grayson suggested. "Doc Hancock might be able to pull some strings and speed up things with a sperm bank. Or I could talk to my brothers. They might know—"

"Don't involve your brothers," Eve interrupted.

Anything but that. Just talking about this

would be hard enough for Grayson, especially telling them that he had turned her down. Eve didn't want to be the subject of conversation at the Ryland dinner table.

"Best not to involve anyone from Silver Creek," she added. "I'll go to a hospital in San Antonio and, well, beg." And she would. This pregnancy was going to happen, even if she didn't have a clue how she would manage it.

She stepped around him and hurried to the driver's side of the car. Since she wasn't looking at Grayson, that was probably the reason she saw the movement.

In the cluster of trees about fifty yards from her car.

"What?" Grayson asked when she froze.

Eve looked around the trees, trying to figure out what had caught her attention.

There.

She saw the man.

Dressed in a dark shirt and pants, he had a black baseball cap sitting low on his head so that it obstructed his face. He quickly ducked out of sight, but from just that quick glimpse, Eve recognized him.

"That's the same man I saw earlier, by the creek," she told Grayson.

Grayson drew his gun from the shoulder holster beneath his jacket. The metal whispered against the leather, and he moved in front of her. "Any idea who he is?"

"No." But she knew that he was hiding, and that couldn't be good.

Did this have anything to do with the hang-up calls she'd been getting? Or could it be her imagination working overtime? Everything suddenly seemed to be going against her.

"I'm Sheriff Grayson Ryland," Grayson called out. "Identify yourself."

Eve stood there and held her breath, waiting. But the man said nothing.

"You think it's a local kid playing a prank?" she whispered, praying that was all there was to this.

Grayson fastened his attention to those trees. "No. A local kid would have answered me."

True. Grayson commanded, and got, respect in Silver Creek. And that caused her heart to pound against her chest. After all, there was a killer on the loose. Eve almost hoped this was connected to the hang-up calls. Better that than having a killer just yards away.

Grayson lifted his gun, and he took aim. "Well?" he prompted, his voice loud enough that the person hiding wouldn't have any trouble hearing him. "Come out so I can see who you are."

Still nothing.

"Get in your car," Grayson instructed from over his shoulder. "I'll get a closer look."

Eve wanted to latch on to him, to stop him from walking toward those trees, but this was his job. Plus, Grayson wouldn't stop. Not for her. Not for anyone.

"Just be careful," she whispered, her voice cracking a little. Eve eased open her car door and ducked down to get inside.

The sound stopped her.

It was a loud blast, and it shook the ground beneath them. Her stomach went to her knees, and her breath stalled in her throat. For a split second she thought someone had shot at them.

But this was much louder than a gunshot.

"Get down!" Grayson shouted.

He didn't give her a chance to do that on her own. He hooked his arm around her waist and pulled her behind her car door and to the ground.

Eve glanced behind her, at the cottage, and she saw what had caused that nightmarish sound.

An explosion.

Her grandmother's cottage was on fire.

Chapter 3

What the hell was going on?

That was Grayson's first thought, quickly followed by the realization that if Eve and he had stayed inside the house just a few more minutes, they would have both been blown to bits.

Behind them, the cottage had orangey flames shooting from it, and there was debris plunging to the ground. Maybe a propane tank had exploded or something, but Grayson wasn't sure it was an accident.

After all, there was a guy hiding in the trees.

Grayson figured it was too much to hope that the two things weren't related.

Had this person somehow rigged the explosion? If so, that meant the man would have had to have gotten close enough to the cottage to tamper with the tank that was just outside the kitchen window, but Grayson hadn't heard him. Of course, he'd been so involved with Eve's baby bombshell that he might not have noticed a tornado bearing down on them. He would berate himself for that later.

Now, he had to do something to protect Eve.

Grayson took cover in front of her and behind the car door, and he re-aimed his gun in the direction of the person he'd seen just moments before the explosion.

"Get out here!" he shouted to the person.

After hearing no response to his last demand, Grayson didn't expect the guy to comply this time. And he didn't.

No answer.

No sign of him.

Grayson kept watch behind them to make sure no one was coming at them from that direction. Other than the falling debris, the fire and black smoke smearing against the sky, there was nothing.

Except Eve, of course.

Her eyes were wide with fear, and he could feel her breath whipping against his back and neck. "We could have died," she mumbled.

Yeah. They'd been damn lucky. A few minutes wasn't much of a window between life and death, and her storming out had literally saved them.

Because she looked to be on the verge of panicking, Grayson wanted to reassure her that all would be fine, but he had no idea if that was true. The one thing he did know was that it wasn't a good idea for them to be in the open like this. There could be a secondary explosion, and he needed to get Eve someplace safe so he could try to figure out what had just happened.

He glanced at his truck, but it was a good thirty feet away. Too far. He didn't want Eve to be out in the open that long. There wasn't just the worry of a second explosion but of their tree-hiding *friend* and what he might try to do.

"Get inside your car," he told Eve, "and slide into the passenger's seat so I can drive."

"Oh, God," he heard her say.

And Grayson silently repeated it. He didn't know just how bad this situation could get, and he didn't want to find out with Eve in tow.

"Put the keys in the ignition," Grayson added when he felt her scramble to get into the car. "And stay down. Get on the floor."

No *Oh, God* this time, but he heard her breath shiver as it rushed past her lips. He wasn't exactly an old pro at facing potentially lethal situations, but he had the training and some experience during his time as sheriff. This had to be a first for Eve.

Not too many people had ever come this close to dying.

Grayson glanced behind him to make sure she had followed his orders. She had. Eve had squeezed herself in between the passenger's seat and the dashboard. It was safer than sitting upright, but Grayson knew a car wouldn't be much protection if anything was about to happen. A secondary explosion could send fiery debris slamming right into them.

He tried to keep watch all around them while he eased into the driver's seat and adjusted it so he'd fit. He needed to put some distance between the cottage, woods and them, and then he would call for assistance. Someone could take Eve to the sheriff's office, and Grayson could figure out why all of this didn't feel like an accident.

While keeping a firm grip on his gun, he shut the car door and started the engine. He took out his phone and handed it to Eve. "Call the fire department."

She did but without taking her stunned gaze off the flames that were eating their way through what was left of the cottage. It had to break her heart to see the damage, and later the full loss would hit her.

As if she hadn't had enough to deal with for one day.

Even now, with the chaos of the moment, he still had her request going through his head.

I need you to get me pregnant.

He'd made it clear that wasn't going to happen, so the situation was over for him. But not for Eve. He had seen that determination in her eyes, and one way or another, she was going to get this dream baby. Hell, this near-death experience might even make her more determined.

"Hang on," Grayson warned her as he drove away—fast. He didn't exactly gun the engine, but he didn't dawdle, either.

The narrow road was dirt, gravel and mud since it had rained hard just that morning. With the sinkholes poxing the surface, it was impossible to have a smooth ride. But a smooth ride was an insignificant concern. Right now, he just wanted Eve out of there so he could deal with this situation on his own terms.

In other words, *alone.*

"The gas was turned off," Eve murmured. "It's been turned off for months. So what caused the explosion?"

"Maybe a leak in the gas line." And if so, that would be easy to prove.

"Call the first number on my contact list," Grayson instructed. It was for the emergency dispatcher in the sheriff's building. "I want at least one deputy out here with the fire department. Have them meet me at the end of the road."

Once help arrived, he could hand off Eve to whichever deputy responded, and Grayson could escort the fire department and others to the scene. He didn't want anyone walking into a potential ambush.

Eve made the call, and he heard her relay his instructions to the emergency dispatcher. Just ahead, Grayson spotted the first curve of the snaky road. He touched the brakes.

And nothing happened.

Nothing!

The car continued to barrel toward the curve. So Grayson cursed and tried again, but this time he added a lot more pressure.

Still nothing.

Hell.

"What's wrong?" Eve asked.

Grayson dropped his gun onto the console between them so he could use both hands to steer. "I think someone cut the brake line."

Eve put her hand against her chest. "W-hat?"

She sounded terrified and probably was, but Grayson couldn't take the time to reassure her that he was going to try to get them out of this without them being hurt. The curve was just seconds away, and the road surface was as slick as spit. But his biggest concern was the trees. The road was lined with them, and if he crashed into one of them, Eve and he could both be killed on impact.

"Get in the seat and put on your seat belt," he told her, fastening his attention on the curve.

She scrambled to do just that, but he figured there wasn't enough time. To buy them a little more of that precious time, Grayson lifted the emergency brake lever, even though it wouldn't help much. The emergency brake would only work on the rear brake, and it wouldn't slow them down enough. Still, he had to try anything to reduce the speed.

"Hold on," he warned her.

Eve was still fumbling with the seat belt when the car went into the curve. Grayson had no choice but to try to keep the vehicle on the road since the trees were just yards away.

The right tires caught the gravel-filled shoulder, kicking up rocks against the metal undercarriage. The sound was nearly deafening, and it blended with his own heartbeat, which was pounding in his ears.

Eve's car went into a slide, the back end fishtailing. Grayson steered into the slide. Or rather that's what he tried to do, but he soon learned he had zero control. He saw the trees getting closer and closer, and there wasn't a damn thing he could do about it.

For just a split second, he made eye contact with Eve. Her gaze was frozen on him while her hands worked frantically to fasten the seat belt. Her eyes said it all.

She thought they were going to die, and she was silently saying goodbye.

Grayson didn't say goodbye back because he had no intention of dying today.

He heard the click of her seat belt, finally. And Grayson jerked the steering wheel to the left. The car careened in that direction, but not before the back end smashed into a live oak tree. The jolt rattled the entire vehicle and tossed them around like rag dolls.

Thank God they were wearing their seat belts.

He also thanked God that he was able to hang on to the steering wheel. They'd dodged a head-on collision, and the impact with the tree had slowed them down some, but they literally weren't out of the woods yet.

The car went into a skid in the opposite direction.

More trees.

Grayson didn't even bother to curse. He just focused all his energy on trying to control an out-of-control car.

And it was a battle he was losing.

There was a trio of hackberry trees directly in front of them. If he managed to miss one, he would no doubt just plow into the others, or one of their low-hanging limbs.

He fought with the wheel, trying to make it turn away, but they were in another skid, the mud and rocks helping to propel them in a direction he didn't want to go.

"There's the man we saw earlier," Eve said, her voice filled with fear.

She pointed to Grayson's right, but he didn't look in that direction. Not because he doubted her. No. The hiding man probably was there, but Grayson had to give it one last-ditch effort to get the car into the best position for what would almost certainly be a collision.

"Cover your face," Grayson managed to warn her. Because the limbs would probably break the glass.

His life didn't exactly flash before his eyes, but Grayson did think of his family. His brothers. His little niece, Kimmie.

And Eve.

She was there, right smack-dab in the middle of all of his memories.

He watched the front end of the car slide toward the middle tree, but at the last second, the vehicle shifted. No longer head-on. But the driver's side—his side—careened right into the hackberry.

Grayson felt the air bags slam into his face and side. The double impact combined with the collision rammed him into Eve and her air bag. There were the sounds of broken glass and the metal crunching against the tree trunk. The radiator spewed steam.

"We're alive," he heard Eve say.

Grayson did a quick assessment. Yeah, they were alive all right, and the car was wrapped around the hackberry.

"Are you hurt?" he asked Eve, trying to assess if he had any injuries of his own. His shoulder hurt like hell, but he was hoping it was just from the air-bag punch and that it hadn't been dislocated. He would need that shoulder to try to get them out of this crumpled heap of a car.

When Eve didn't answer, Grayson's stomach knotted, and he whipped his head in her direction. Her hands were on the air bag that she was trying to bat down, but her attention was fixed on the side window.

Grayson soon saw why.

The man, the one who'd hidden in the trees, was running straight toward them.

Chapter 4

The man was armed, a pistol in his right hand.

Eve heard Grayson yell for her to get down, but she didn't have time to react. Grayson pushed her down, her face and body colliding with the partially inflated air bag.

"My gun," he snarled.

Grayson cursed and punched at the air bags. He was obviously trying to find his weapon. When Eve had last seen it, Grayson had put it on the console, but the crash had probably sent it flying.

Oh, mercy.

That meant they were sitting ducks, unarmed, with a gunman bearing down on them. She couldn't get out of the car, not with the man so close and on her side of the vehicle. They couldn't get out on the driver's side because it was literally crunched around a tree. Thank God for the air bags, or Grayson would have been seriously injured or killed.

Eve glanced up at the approaching man. The person who was likely responsible for the explosion that had destroyed her grandmother's cottage. The fear raced through her.

Still, she felt anger, too.

This idiot had endangered them and was continuing to do so. She wouldn't just stand by and let him shoot Grayson and her. Neither would Grayson.

They both grappled around the interior of her car, and Eve remembered her own gun in the glove compartment. It took some doing to get the air bag out of the way, but she finally managed it. She threw open the glove box door, latched on to the gun and handed it to Grayson.

He immediately took aim.

The man must have seen him do that because he ducked behind a tree. She wasn't sure if that was a good or bad thing. If the man had stayed out in the open, Grayson would have had a clean shot. This way, they were still trapped.

"One of the deputies will be here soon," Grayson reminded her.

Probably one of his brothers. Both Dade and Mason were Silver Creek deputy sheriffs, and since Grayson had requested backup, they would no doubt get there as soon as humanly possible.

But that might not be soon enough.

Using his left hand Grayson continued to bat away the air bag, but he kept his attention pinned to the tree where the man had ducked out of sight. Eve kept watch as well, but there were other trees near that one, and it wouldn't take much for the man to move behind one of those closer trees and sneak right up on them.

"Who is he?" Eve meant to ask herself that question, but she said it aloud.

"I don't know," Grayson answered. "But he could be the killer we're after."

Yes. Eve was aware that there was an unidentified killer on the loose.

Thanks to the newspaper coverage, she was also aware that just a few days ago a young woman's body had been found in the creek. The woman had been fully clothed, no signs of sexual assault, but her fingerprints and face had been obliterated. That's the term the press had used, *obliterated,* and Eve had assumed the killer had done that to prevent her from being identified.

It had worked.

So why would this killer come after Grayson and her now?

Until the body was identified, and that might never happen, it wasn't likely that Grayson would be able to come up with a list of suspects.

But Eve had a sickening thought.

Perhaps the man had killed the woman in or near the cottage. Maybe he was destroying any potential physical evidence that would link him to the crime. And here she'd walked in with so much on her mind that she hadn't even considered a trip home could be dangerous. This in spite of her knowing about the murder that possibly happened just a stone's throw away from the cottage.

That oversight could be deadly.

She choked back a sob. Only minutes earlier her main worry had been getting pregnant, but for that to happen Grayson and she had to survive this. If something went wrong and he got hurt, it would be her fault because he wouldn't have been out here in these woods if she hadn't called him.

"I'll get you out of here," she heard Grayson say.

It sounded like a promise. But Eve knew backup was still a few minutes away. A lot could happen in those few short minutes.

Because she had her attention pinned to that tree, she saw the man lean out. Or rather she saw his gun.

"Get down!" she warned Grayson.

Just as the shot slammed through the window directly above Eve's head. The sound was deafening, and the bullet tore through the safety glass.

Grayson moved forward, his body and forearm pushing her deeper onto the floor so that she could no longer see what was going on.

And Grayson fired.

Eve automatically put her hands over her ears, but the blast was so loud that it seemed to shake the entire car. What was left of the safety glass in the window came tumbling down on top of her.

Grayson elbowed the chunk of glass aside and fired another shot. All Eve could do was pray, and her prayers were quickly answered. Even with the roaring in her ears from the shots, she heard a welcome sound.

A siren.

Maybe the fire department. Maybe a deputy. She didn't care which. She just wanted Grayson to have backup. Her gun was fully loaded, but Eve didn't have any other ammunition with her, and she didn't want to risk a gun battle with the man who had a better position behind the tree.

"The SOB's getting away," Grayson growled.

Eve hadn't thought this situation could get more frightening, but that did it. If he managed to escape, he might try to come after her again.

She didn't need this, and neither did Grayson.

Grayson obviously agreed because he climbed over her and caught on to the door handle. He turned it, but it didn't budge. Eve didn't relish the idea of Grayson running after a possible killer, but the alternative was worse. Besides, the gunman had quit shooting.

For now, anyway.

Eve rammed her weight against the door to help Grayson open it. It took several hard pushes, but with their combined effort the door finally flew open.

"Be careful," she warned him.

"You, too," Grayson warned back. "Stay put and try to find my gun. I figure he's trying to get as far away from that siren as he can, but if this guy is stupid and doubles back, shoot him."

That didn't help with her ragged nerves, but

as Grayson sprang from the car, Eve made a frantic search for the gun. She also kept watch, blindly running her hands over the floor and seats.

The sirens got closer, and she saw the flashes of blue lights at the end of the road. Backup was just seconds away, but Grayson was already running past the tree that the gunman had hidden behind.

Her fingers brushed over the cold gunmetal, finally, and Eve snatched up Grayson's Smith & Wesson. Her hands were shaking like crazy, but she positioned the gun so it would be easier for her to take aim. But she was hoping that might not be necessary.

A Silver Creek cruiser came to a screeching stop next to her wrecked car, and she recognized the man who jumped out. It was Dade, Grayson's brother. Like Grayson, he wore jeans and a badge clipped to his belt, and he had his gun ready. He was lankier than Grayson, but Eve didn't doubt Dade's capabilities. From everything she'd heard, he was a good lawman.

"Eve?" he asked. Dade was clearly surprised to see her in Silver Creek. Then his gaze flashed to the cottage. Or rather what remained of it. It was still on fire, but there wasn't much left to burn.

Soon, very soon, it would be just a pile of ashes.

"Someone blew up the cottage. And then he fired a shot at us," she explained. "He might be the killer you're looking for." Mercy, her voice was shaking as badly as her hands, and she tried to rein in her fear so she could point toward the tree. "Grayson went after him."

Concern flashed through Dade's eyes, and he snapped his attention in the direction where she'd pointed. "Stay here," Dade said, repeating Grayson's earlier order. "The fire crew is right behind me. And keep that gun ready, just in case."

She watched him run toward the spot where she'd last seen Grayson, and Eve added another prayer for Dade's safety, too. Like all the Rylands, she'd known Dade her entire life, and even though he was only two years younger than she was, she had always thought of him as her kid brother. That probably had something to do with all the meals she'd helped cook for Dade and the others after their mother committed suicide.

"The dark ages," she mumbled.

That's how she'd always thought of that time twenty years ago when Grayson and his brothers had basically become orphans. During the years that followed, Eve had gotten close with all of Grayson's brothers, closer than she had been with her own family.

She blinked back the tears. And here she'd endangered yet another *family* member. Heck, Mason was probably on the way, too. Before the hour was up, she might have put all three of them at risk.

Eve heard a second set of sirens and knew that the fire department was close by. She stayed in the car, as both Grayson and Dade had warned her to do, but she moved to the edge of the seat, closer to the open door, so she could try to pick through the woods and see Grayson. She still had sight of Dade, but Grayson was nowhere to be seen.

She glanced behind her at the fire engine as it made the final turn from the farm road onto the gravel drive that led to the cottage. The driver turned off the sirens, and everything suddenly went silent.

Eve could hear the wind assaulting the trees. She could hear her own heartbeat in her ears.

She also heard Dade shout, "Get down!"

And the sound of a gun going off ripped through the silence.

Chapter 5

Grayson cursed and dove to the ground.

He'd already had enough surprises today, and he didn't need this SOB firing any more shots at him. Besides, Eve wasn't that far away, and he darn sure didn't want a stray bullet traveling in her direction.

"You okay?" Dade called out. His brother had dropped to the ground, too, but was crawling toward Grayson.

"Yeah. I'm just fine and dandy," Grayson barked. "You see him?"

Dade didn't answer right away, giving Grayson some hope, but that hope went south when his brother finally said, "No."

Grayson lifted his head and examined the

woods. Since it was the dead of winter, a lot of the foliage was gone, but that didn't mean there weren't plenty of places to hide.

And then Grayson heard something he didn't want to hear.

The sound of water.

Hell. This guy was in the creek, and that meant he was getting away.

Dade apparently heard it, too, because he cursed and got to his feet. So did Grayson, and they started to run toward the sound of that splashing. Of course, the splashing was long gone before they arrived on the creek bank.

And there was no sign of the gunman.

Dade and Grayson stood there, looking hard, but there was no way to tell which direction he went. If the guy was smart, he could have just floated downstream and out of sight. Of course, he could have scrambled over the outcropping of rocks on the other side of the creek bed and then disappeared into the dense woods.

"We need a tracking dog," Dade mumbled.

Yeah. And they needed their brother Mason out here on horseback. Mason was a better tracker than any dog or any of the local Texas Rangers, but Grayson intended to ask for their help, too. He wanted this gunman caught *now,* and he would use any resource available.

"I got a good look at his face," Grayson let Dade know. "If he's in the system, I think I can pick out his photo."

Though that would take time. Maybe lots of time. Something Grayson wasn't sure he had.

This guy would be back.

The question was why? Grayson was sure if he could figure that out, then he would have a better chance of identifying him and stopping another attack.

"Why don't you get Eve away from here? She's pretty shaken up," Dade suggested. He took out his cell phone. "I'll start making calls."

Grayson started to say no, that he wanted to stay. If they got lucky with the search, he wanted to be the one to put the cuffs on this piece of slime, but Dade was right. Eve didn't need to be here. Neither did he. His brothers could handle it and handle it well. So he turned and headed back toward Eve and her car.

He spotted her the moment he came out of the thick cluster of trees. She was out of the wrecked car, talking to Dusty Bullock, the fire chief. She looked calm enough, but Grayson knew that underneath her nerves had to be raw since to the best of his knowledge this was the first time she'd experienced anyone trying to kill her.

And there was no doubt that the killing attempt had been aimed at Eve.

When she saw Grayson, Eve ran toward him, but he quickly closed the distance between them because he didn't want her out in the open.

"Did you catch him?" she asked.

Grayson shook his head and watched her expression go from shock to fear. Yeah. She understood how important it was for them to find this gunman *today*.

Since she looked ready to launch herself into his arms, or cry, he took his gun from her, reholstered it and handed Eve her handgun. She slipped it into her coat pocket. And Grayson caught on to her shoulder so he could lead her in the direction of his truck.

"I need to get you back to my office," he grumbled. Grayson hated the gruffness in his voice. Hated even more that he couldn't comfort her at a time when she needed comforting, but after the conversation they'd had in the cottage, it was best if he kept his distance.

"But what about the gunman?" she challenged. "He's still out there."

"Dade's looking for him, and we'll bring in help." Grayson stopped next to the fire chief.

"Call me the minute you know what caused the explosion in the cottage."

"You're thinking it was foul play?" Dusty asked, his craggy face bunched up with concern.

"Yeah," Grayson answered honestly, though he knew that would cause Eve more panic. "I want the brake line on Eve's car checked, too, because I'm sure someone cut it."

"Oh, God," Eve mumbled.

He got her moving again, but she stopped first to retrieve her purse and equipment bag from her car. Since she looked ready to fall apart, Grayson decided to use the drive to his office to get her to concentrate on how they could bring this nightmarish day to a good conclusion.

A conclusion that would end with an arrest.

"Did you see the gunman's face?" Grayson asked. He drove away from her cottage, which would soon be taped off and processed as a crime scene.

"Not really." When she couldn't get her seat belt on after two tries, Grayson reached over and helped her. His hand brushed against hers, and he quickly pulled back. With the energy between them already on edge, it was best to avoid touching her.

And *thinking* about touching her.

Something he didn't quite accomplish.

Grayson huffed and continued. "The gunman had brownish-red hair. About six-two. Around a hundred and seventy pounds. Ring any bells?"

She shook her head. "Should it?"

"Maybe. I figure you've crossed paths with him. Why else would he want to come after you that way?"

Eve mumbled another "Oh, God," and plowed her fingers through the sides of her hair. "I don't recognize him." She pressed hard against her temples and head. "What could I have done to make him want to kill me?"

That was the million-dollar question, and Grayson had to explore all possibilities. "An old boyfriend, maybe? Maybe he altered his appearance so that you didn't easily recognize him?"

Her hands slipped from her hair and dropped into her lap. She stared at him. "You're the only boyfriend I have who's riled at me."

"I'm not riled," Grayson protested.

She huffed. "You're riled all right."

He huffed, too. "Just because I turned down your offer to make a baby doesn't mean I'm pissed off." But when he heard his tone, he realized he was. Grayson cursed. "I just wasn't expecting you to ask anything like that, okay? You surprised the hell out of me."

"Yes, I figured that out. But you can't blame me for trying. I just thought… Well, I just thought *wrong*."

She was right about that. So, why did Grayson feel so blasted guilty for turning her down? Since that was something he didn't want to think or talk about, he went back to the investigation. They were still fifteen minutes out from his office, and he wanted to put that time to good use instead of adding to that guilt trip.

"I heard you were engaged but broke things off," Grayson tossed out there. "Could your ex be holding a grudge?"

She mumbled something he didn't catch. "No. It's true, I called things off the day of the wedding, but he's moved on and already married to someone else."

Maybe her ex-fiancé had indeed moved on, but Grayson wanted to verify that was true. Love and love-scorned were motives for a lot of crimes.

And a lot of questions.

He wanted to ask Eve why she'd waited until her wedding day to end things, but it was none of his business.

"How about a member of your ex's family?" he pressed. "Sometimes family members or friends think they need to avenge a broken heart."

She sat quietly a moment. And she didn't deny that broken heart part. "Why wait over a year to get revenge?" She shook her head again. "I was thinking maybe what happened today has to do with the killer. Maybe he was trying to destroy evidence by destroying the cottage?"

Yes. That was the next theory on Grayson's list. Perhaps the killer had left some kind of forensic evidence in or near the cottage. That was a solid reason to destroy it.

"But then why would he want to kill you?" Grayson pressed. He turned off the ranch road and onto the highway that would take him back into town. "Is it possible you know something about the murder?"

"How could I? I wasn't in Silver Creek when it happened. I was in San Antonio."

"The murder might not have happened in Silver Creek," he reminded her. "In fact, I suspect it didn't. I think the body was just dumped there."

She gave him a flat look. "Trust me, I would have remembered if I'd witnessed someone being murdered."

True. But there had to be a reason this guy

was after her. Grayson really needed to get an ID on that body because he couldn't shake the feeling that the dead woman and this attack were connected.

"We don't have an identity on the dead woman, but she was five-six and was in her early twenties." Grayson hoped that would spur Eve to remember something.

Eve nodded. "I read that in the paper. Her face and fingerprints had been obliterated." She paused. "What does that mean exactly?"

"You don't want to know." But Grayson would never forget the sight of what was left of the woman. Someone had literally bashed in her face so that none of her features had been recognizable, and then cut off the pads of her fingertips. He'd also broken off her teeth, probably so that dental records couldn't be used to identify her. "But the killer didn't obliterate her hair, and it's unique. Three colors—red, black and blond. Remember seeing anyone with hair like that?"

She shrugged. "It's possible. That type of hair isn't so rare in a city the size of San Antonio."

True. But it was the only thing he had to go on. Now it was time to grasp at a few straws. "When did you start getting hang-up calls?" Grayson pressed.

"Four days ago," she answered without hesitation.

Four days. According to the ME, that was an estimate of when the woman had been killed.

He was about to continue his questions when Grayson spotted the familiar rust-scabbed red truck barreling down the highway. It was his brother Mason, responding to the scene. Grayson didn't slow down. Neither did Mason. They exchanged a glance, and in that split-second glance, Grayson saw exactly what he wanted to see: Mason's determination to find the man who'd taken shots at Eve and him.

Sometimes keeping Mason's intense moods under control was like trying to keep a leash on a rogue bull. But it was that intensity that made Mason a good cop. Mason wasn't the sort of man Grayson would go to with his personal problems—he wouldn't get much empathy there—but for everything else Mason was the brother he knew he could rely on the most.

Grayson stopped in the parking lot of his office and turned to Eve. "I need to get your statement about what just happened and ask you a few more questions about those hang-up calls. Then I can take you to the ranch. You can stay there until we catch this guy."

She was already shaking her head before he finished. "I can't go to your ranch."

No. He didn't have time for this argument. "Look, I know it might be a little uncomfortable for you there, what with Dade and Mason around—"

"It's not that. I'm comfortable with your family. Always have been."

Grayson couldn't argue with that. Heck, his brothers had, and probably always would, consider Eve a sister. His youngest brother, Kade, often said that Eve was more like a mother to him than his own mother had been.

So what was Eve's issue?

She stared at him. "I need to get back to San Antonio, and I intend to do that as soon as I can arrange for transportation. Your reports will have to wait. I have to find a place where I can be inseminated *today.*"

Grayson was sure he looked at her as if she'd lost her mind. "Eve, someone tried to kill you," he reminded her, though he was positive she hadn't forgotten that.

Her hand was still shaking when she touched her fingers to her lips. She paused a moment, still trembling, and her gaze came back to his. "If I don't do the insemination today, I'll never have a baby. And yes, I know there's a killer out there. And yes, that killer might have been the one to take shots at us today. But I don't have time to wait for him to be caught."

Grayson broke his no-touching rule and caught on to her shoulders. He wanted to make this very clear. But for a moment he lost his train of thought when he saw the nicks and scrapes on her face. From the air bag, no doubt. But even with the superficial damage, Eve was still the most beautiful woman he'd ever seen.

He pushed that thought aside with all the rest of the carnal things that came to mind whenever he looked at Eve. She had, and always would have, his number.

Grayson met her eye to eye. "The killer could come after you in San Antonio."

She blinked, swallowed hard. "So, I'll hire a bodyguard as soon as I call the rental car company to come and get me. I want to be on the road within the next thirty minutes."

He didn't know whether to curse or try to shake some sense into her. "Eve, is this baby worth your life?"

Her breath rattled in her throat. Tears sprang to her eyes. "Yes," she whispered.

And with that, she grabbed her equipment bag and purse and got out of his truck. The bag went on one shoulder. Her purse on the other.

Well, he'd asked the question, and even though it hadn't been the answer he wanted to hear, Grayson knew it was Eve's final answer. She wasn't going to budge on this.

Hell.

That meant he had to drive back into San Antonio with her. Or else send Dade or Mason. Now Grayson cursed because he sure didn't have time for this.

He got out, slammed the truck door with far more force than necessary and followed her into the back entrance of the law enforcement building. It wasn't a huge place—especially considering how much time he spent there. It had a reception area, four offices, two interrogation rooms and a holding cell on the bottom floor. There was an apartment-style break room on the top floor where there'd once been jail cells before a new facility had been built on the edge of town.

Grayson stepped inside and heard the day shift dispatcher, Tina Fox, talking from her desk in the reception area. An area roped off with twinkling Christmas lights and a miniature tree that played annoying tinny carols when anyone walked past it. Mason had already kicked it once. Grayson was considering the same. As far as he was concerned, this was a bah-humbug kind of Christmas, and this attempt to kill Eve wasn't doing much to change his opinion about that.

Tina looked back at him and waved. From the sound of it, she was getting an update from Dade. Soon Grayson would want that update as well, but first he had to deal with the most hardheaded woman in Texas.

Ahead of him, Eve made her way to his office while she fished for something in her purse. She finally pulled out her cell phone when she came to a quick stop. Her hand and phone had been moving toward her ear, but that stopped, as well. She stood there frozen, her gaze fixed on something in his office.

Grayson cursed and hurried to pull her aside because he knew what had shocked her. The crime board in his office had photos of the dead woman. Or rather what was left of her. To put it mildly, they weren't pretty.

"Sorry about that," he mumbled. And he crossed the room to turn the board around so that the gruesome pictures would be facing the wall.

"Wait!" Eve insisted.

She walked closer, her attention nailed to the grisliest of the photos. It was a close-up view of the dead woman's bashed-in face and had been taken several hours after her body had been fished out of the creek.

"There's no need for you to see these," Grayson assured her. When he tried to turn the board again, she caught on to his arm to stop them.

She moved even closer, until her face was just inches from the photo. Eve mumbled something and then dropped her equipment bag onto his desk. Frantically, she began to rummage through it, pulling out the pictures that Grayson had seen earlier on the counter at the cottage.

"What is it?" he asked.

"I've seen her before." Her voice was all breath now. "Well, I've seen that hair anyway."

Grayson glanced back at the dead woman's hair, though the image was already embedded into his mind. He wasn't sure he'd ever be able to forget it. But the hair was certainly distinctive. Three colors. Red, blond, black, and the black was only on the ends of her choppily cut hair.

Eve continued to pull photos from her bag, glancing at each and then tossing them aside on the tops of folders and reports that Grayson had spread out on his desk. She plucked another from the bag and froze again.

Grayson looked at the shot from over her shoulder. He recognized the location—it had been taken at the indoor rodeo arena in San

Antonio. There were at least a dozen people standing at the railings, their eyes fixed on the bull rider who had just been tossed into the air.

Then he saw the woman.

And her hair.

"When did you take this?" Grayson couldn't ask the question fast enough. He grabbed the picture from her so he could study it.

"Four days ago at the fund-raiser rodeo. I had these printed because I wanted to take a better look at them to see which to include in the story. But I didn't use this one." She paused. "It's her, isn't it?"

Grayson paused, too, but not because he wasn't sure.

He was.

The image of the dead woman stared back at him.

Chapter 6

Eve hadn't realized she was holding her breath until her lungs began to ache. "Is that the murdered woman?" she asked Grayson.

"Yeah," he finally said, his attention still glued to that photo. "Any idea who she is?"

"No, I took dozens of random shots that day. She was just someone in the crowd."

"Yes. But if the medical examiner is right, this is also the day she was murdered." He tipped his head to her bag. "I need to look at all the pictures."

She gave a shaky nod, and while she was doing that, Grayson peeled off his jacket and tossed it over the back of his chair. Then he put the photo on his fax machine. "I'm send-

ing it to the Ranger crime lab in Austin with
a request for immediate processing."

Good. Soon he might have a name to go
with that face.

Eve continued to dump pictures onto his
desk, but with each one she mumbled a no. She
huffed. "That's it. The only one I have of her."

"Then I'll have to get what I can from it."

He made several more copies of the picture,
one that he pinned on to the corkboard with the
other photos. The others, he put in his in-basket
so he'd have them for other law enforcement
agencies. Then he sat at his desk, placing the
original picture right next to him, and he fired
off that request message to the Ranger crime
lab.

While he did that, Eve took herself back to
that photo session. It had been routine, something she'd done dozens of times.

"Four days ago," she said softly. "That's
when my hang-up calls started."

That got Grayson's attention. He stood
and stared at her, and Eve knew what he was
thinking. Was there something in the photo
that had caused the hang-up calls, the fire at
the cottage and the shooting?

Was the killer in the photo?

Eve rifled through her equipment bag and

came up with a small magnifying glass. She handed it to Grayson, and he used it to zoom in. She hurried beside him so she could take a look, as well.

Unlike the rest of the spectators, the woman wasn't looking at the bull rider. She had her attention on the man wearing a baseball cap on her left. Her face was tight, as if she was angry. *Very* angry. And the man had his hand gripped on to her arm.

"I'm pretty sure that's the guy who shot at us today," Grayson mumbled, tapping his finger to the guy in the baseball cap.

Eve sucked in her breath. She hadn't gotten a good look at him, but the build was right. So was that baseball cap.

Grayson turned back to his keyboard. "I'll ask the lab to put the entire picture into the facial recognition program. It's the fastest way for us to get an ID."

Good. Eve wanted that. But she also wanted to get out of there and on the road. It was already past noon, and time was running out. She took out her cell to call for a car rental, but before she could make the call, Grayson's phone rang.

"Sheriff Ryland," he answered, and she knew from his expression that whoever was on the other end of the line was telling him something important. Was it possible the Rangers had already managed to ID the dead woman? Eve prayed they had. Because the sooner that happened, the sooner Grayson could proceed with the investigation.

"Yeah. I'll let Eve know," Grayson mumbled several seconds later. "What about the search? Any sign of the gunman?" He paused. "Keep looking."

"What happened?" she asked the moment he hung up.

"That was the fire chief." Grayson pulled in a long breath. "He said he's positive someone tampered with both your brakes and the gas line that led to the cottage. Plus, there was a tracking device on your car."

Eve had tried to brace herself for bad news. After all, it was a logical conclusion about the brakes and gas line, but it still sent an icy chill through her. So did the fact that someone had tracked her out to the cottage.

God, did someone really want her dead because she'd taken a photo?

"Do you park your car in a garage in San Antonio?" Grayson asked.

"No. I use the lot adjacent to my condo."

In other words, her vehicle had been out in

the open. Not just there but at her downtown office, as well. Obviously, someone could have planted that tracking device at any time in the past four days. And during those four days, the person had no doubt watched her, plotting the best way to get the picture and eliminate her.

She held on to Grayson's desk to steady herself.

Grayson cursed, moved out of his chair, grabbed her arm and forced her to sit down. "I hope now you realize that going back to San Antonio is a bad idea."

Yes. She did. But that wouldn't stop her. "Then I'll go to Austin. I'm sure they have fertility clinics there."

Grayson didn't curse again, but the look he gave her showed the profanity he was choking back.

"I don't expect you to understand." She got to her feet and squared her shoulders. She looked him straight in the eye. "You're burned out with the whole idea of fatherhood so how could you understand that for me having a baby, *my* baby, is the most important thing in my life?"

Grayson looked her straight in the eyes, too. "Eve, what I understand is this killer knows you took his picture, and he'll do anything to

get it back. I can keep you safe here in Silver
Creek until we can get the picture printed in
tomorrow's paper. That way, the killer won't
have a reason to come after you because thousands of people will have seen his face, along
with the woman he probably murdered."

She tried to shrug. Eve wasn't immune to
the fear, but she wasn't giving in to it, either.
"Then print the photo, and tomorrow I can celebrate both my insemination and my safety."

He didn't answer that and just kept glaring as if searching for the right argument to
change her mind. There wasn't an argument
that could do that.

Eve adjusted her cell again, ready to make
her call. "I'll get a car rental, and on the drive
to Austin, I'll phone clinics and start begging. One way or another, I'm getting pregnant today."

Now he cursed and shook his head. "Give
me a few minutes, and I'll drive you to Austin myself."

Eve hadn't thought the day could have any
more surprises, but that was a big one, and
she knew just how massive a concession that
was for Grayson.

"You can't," she argued. "You have too
much to do to babysit me."

"Save your breath," he growled. He grabbed

his coat and put it on as if he taking his anger out on the garment. He also snatched the rodeo photo of the dead woman. "You're not the only hardheaded person in this room. And if you can make calls on the drive over, then so can I. If I have to, I'll run this investigation from my truck."

He brushed past her and headed for his door, and she heard him tell the dispatcher that he had to leave. Eve didn't want to think of what kind of complications this might cause for Grayson, but she knew it would. She also knew this was another huge compromise for him. Maybe Dade and Mason could find this gunman today so this would all be over.

She gathered up the pictures and stuffed them into the equipment bag. Her hand knocked against another photo. The only framed one on Grayson's desk. It was of his maternal grandfather, Sheriff Chet McLaurin.

Despite her own horrible circumstances, she smiled when she saw the man's face. Eve had known him well, and he'd become like her own grandfather. When he'd been murdered twenty years ago, Eve had grieved right along with the Ryland clan.

She wondered if Grayson and his brothers realized that the man in the photo was the reason they'd all gotten into law enforcement. An unsolved murder could do that. It was a wound that would not heal.

Eve spotted another wound.

The silver concho hooked on to the top of the frame. She recognized it, as well. Grayson's father had given all six of his sons a concho with the double *R* symbol of their family's ranch. He'd done that, and then less than a week later, he'd left Silver Creek and abandoned the very family that he claimed to have loved.

No wonder Grayson didn't want kids of his own.

He'd witnessed firsthand that parenthood could cut to the core. Eve swore she would never do that to her child.

"Ready?" Grayson said from the doorway.

She'd been so caught up in the picture of his grandfather and the concho that she hadn't noticed Grayson was there. He had also noticed what had caught her attention.

"Yeah," he mumbled as if he'd known exactly what she'd been thinking.

Eve silently cursed the legacy that Grayson's father had left him, and she stuffed the rest of her things into the equipment bag.

"You kept the concho he gave you," she commented as they went to his truck.

He didn't answer until they were both inside the cab of his truck. "Sometimes it helps to remember how much I hate my father."

She stared at him. "How could that possibly help?"

"It's a reminder that sometimes the easy way out can hurt a lot of people."

He didn't look at her when he said that, and if Eve hadn't known him so well she might have thought that was a jab at her decision to go through with this insemination. But since she did know him, she figured he was talking about his family duties. For Grayson, family came first, and that hadn't always been easy for him.

"Mason put a bullet in his concho," Grayson said under his breath. He drove out of the parking lot and onto the road that would take them out of town and to the highway. "Then he nailed it to the wall directly in front of his bed so he could curse it every morning when he woke up."

Eve sighed. So much hurt caused by one man. Their father, Boone Ryland. "I remember Dade told me that he threw his away."

"Yeah." And for a moment, Grayson seemed lost in those bad memories. The dark ages. However, his cell rang, and he morphed from the wounded son to steely sheriff.

"Sheriff Ryland," he answered. He put the phone on speaker and slipped it into a stand that was mounted to the dashboard. He also kept watch around them as they passed the last of the town shops.

"It's me, Dade. I just got off the phone with the Ranger lab. They got a match on the photo."

"Already?" Grayson questioned.

"It wasn't that hard. Her name is Nina Manning, age twenty-two, from Houston, and she had a record for drug possession and prostitution. There's also a year-old missing person's report complete with pictures."

"Nina Manning," Eve repeated. It didn't ring any bells.

"Is Eve still with you?" Dade asked.

Eve looked at Grayson and waited for him to answer. "Yeah. I have to drive her, uh, somewhere. But I want to know everything that's happening with the case. Any sign of the gunman?"

"No. But Mason's out here. If the guy's still in the area, Mason will find him."

Eve doubted the gunman was still around. Heck, he'd probably parked his car on one of the ranch trails and was now probably long gone. Or maybe he was looking for her. Despite the importance of Dade's call, that caused her to look in the rearview mirror. No one was following them. The rural road behind them was empty.

"Were the Rangers able to identify the other man in the picture who had hold of Nina's arm?" Grayson asked.

"There was no immediate match."

Grayson shook his head. "I think he's the guy who tried to kill us today so we need an ID."

"The Rangers are still trying," Dade assured him. "But they did get a match on the man to the woman's right. His name is Sebastian Collier."

Now that rang some bells. Eve had seen the surname many times in the newspaper, mainly in the business and society sections. "He's related to Claude Collier, the San Antonio real estate tycoon?" Eve asked.

"Sebastian is his son," Dade answered. "And sonny-boy has a record, too, for a DWI and resisting arrest. Guess his millionaire daddy didn't teach him to call the family chauffeur when he's had too much to drink."

Eve picked up the photo that Grayson had brought along, and she zoomed in on the man to Nina Manning's right. Sebastian Collier looked like a preppy college student in his collared cream-colored shirt and dark pants. It certainly didn't seem as if he was with the woman with multicolored hair.

But then Eve looked closer.

Sebastian's attention was certainly on Nina. His eyes were angled in her direction, or rather in the direction of the grip the other man had on Nina's arm. Sebastian looked uncomfortable with the encounter.

"Keep pushing the Rangers," she heard Grayson tell his brother. "I want that other man identified. I also want someone out to question this Sebastian Collier." He looked at his watch, mumbled something in disgust. "I'll try to get to San Antonio myself as soon as I'm sure Eve will be safe."

Dade assured Grayson he would do everything to get a name to go with that face in the photo, and he ended the call.

Eve hadn't missed Grayson's mumble of disgust, and she was positive she was the cause. He wanted to be in the heat of this investigation, but here he was driving her to Austin instead. She turned to face him, to tell him that he could just drop her off in Austin and leave. Not that it would do any good—he would insist on staying. But she had to try. This investigation was important to both of them.

However, before she could launch into another argument, she heard the sound.

It was a thick, hard blast.

At first she thought maybe they'd had a blowout. But the second sound was identical.

"Get down!" Grayson shouted.

Just as a third blast ripped through the truck window.

Chapter 7

Grayson slammed his foot onto the accelerator to get Eve and him out of there, but it was already too late.

He heard the fourth shot, and he also heard Eve repeat his shouted command of *get down*. But he couldn't duck out of sight. He had to fight to keep them alive. He pushed Eve down onto the seat so that she wouldn't be hit with the bullet or the broken glass.

But the bullet didn't crash through the glass.

It hit the tire.

Grayson's stomach knotted, and he felt his truck jerk to the right. He fought with the steering wheel and tried to stay on the road, but it was impossible. The now-flat tire and metal rim scraped against the gravel shoulder.

"Hang on," he warned Eve.

They were going to crash.

He couldn't avoid that. However, the crash was the least of Grayson's worries. Someone had shot out the tire, and that someone was no doubt waiting for them. That meant Eve was in danger all over again, and Grayson cursed the bastard responsible for that.

There were no trees near the road, thank God, but there were clusters about a hundred yards off the road. That's probably where the gunman was hiding. And then there was the creek directly in front of them. He didn't want to go there because there were some deep spots in the water that could swallow them up.

"We have to jump," Grayson told her, and he pumped the brakes to slow the truck as much as he could. However, he didn't have much control of the vehicle.

Jumping was a risk, but the greater risk would be to remain inside so the gunman would have an easier chance of killing them. Besides, there was that potential for drowning.

Eve didn't answer, but she nodded and caught on to the door handle.

"When you jump out, run toward the trees to the right," he added. "And grab my cell phone."

Grayson took out his gun. Eve grabbed the phone.

"Now!" He barreled out at the same time as Eve, and he hit the soggy ground ready to fire. The truck gave Eve some cover for just a few seconds, until it plunged nose-first into the creek.

The gunman fired, the shot kicking up mud and a clump of grass several yards in front of Grayson. Grayson returned fire, a single shot, praying it would buy Eve enough time. He could hear her running, but he had to do everything to keep the gunman's attention on him.

Grayson spotted the gunman, or rather the sleeve of his jacket. He spotted Eve, too. She had ducked behind an oak and had taken out her own gun from her coat pocket. She leaned out and took aim at the gunman.

What the hell was she doing?

That knot in his stomach twisted even harder. She had purposely left cover, the very thing he didn't want her to do. Grayson frantically motioned for her to get back. But she didn't. She fired. Her shot slammed into the tree where the gunman was hiding. The bullet didn't hit him, but it caused the man to jump back.

Even though Eve's diversion could have been deadly, it was exactly what Grayson needed because he scrambled toward Eve and dove behind the tree. He also caught on to her and pulled her deeper into the woods. He damn sure didn't want her to get hurt trying to protect him.

"Stay back," Grayson warned her in a rough whisper. But he soon realized that staying back might be just as dangerous as staying put. That's because the gunman was on the move. He dropped back into the thick patch of trees. The SOB was trying to circle behind them.

Grayson had faced danger alone and had even faced it with other lawmen, but being under fire with a civilian was a first. And to make matters worse, that civilian was Eve. He wished he could go back in time and save her from this.

He repositioned Eve behind him and went deeper into the woods as well, but not toward the gunman. They needed to get into a better position, so with Eve in tow, he started moving, going at a right angle. He tried to keep his steps light so that it wouldn't give them away, but that wasn't easy with the dead limbs and leaves littering the grounds.

Eve and he ran, until he lost sight of the road and truck, and he didn't stop until he reached a small clearing.

Another shot came at them.

It wasn't close, at least twenty feet away, but the gunman had sent it in their direction. However, Grayson now knew the gunman's direction, too.

He moved Eve to the right, and they followed the thick woods until they reached the other side of the clearing. Grayson glanced back at Eve to make sure she was okay.

Her breath was gusting now, she was pale, but she didn't appear to be on the verge of panicking. There was some fear there in her eyes, but there was also determination to get out of this alive.

Eve motioned across the clearing, and Grayson saw the gunman duck behind another tree. He caught just a glimpse of the man's face, but Grayson was more convinced than ever that this was the same person in the photo with the dead woman. Grayson hadn't had many doubts left that this was connected to the photograph Eve had taken, and he certainly didn't doubt it now.

The gunman continued to work his way to his right, and Grayson did the same. It was a risk taking Eve deeper and deeper into the woods, but he had to figure out a way to stop this guy. Preferably alive. But he was more than willing to take him out if it meant Eve and he could get out of there.

When they'd made it all the way to a new section of the creek, Grayson stopped and waited.

He didn't have to wait long.

Grayson spotted the gunman just as the man spotted them.

The gunman lifted his weapon, but Grayson was already braced for the attack. He shoved Eve back, took aim and fired before the gunman could. It was a sickening sound of the bullet slamming into human flesh.

A deadly thud.

Clutching his chest, the man flew backward and landed among the dense underbrush.

"Is he...dead?" Eve whispered.

"Maybe." The moments crawled by, and Grayson waited. Watching. He looked for any movement, but he didn't see it. "Stay here."

Eve caught on to his arm and looked ready to launch into an argument about why he should stay put, but her gaze dropped to his badge. Resignation went through her eyes as a worried sigh left her mouth. "Be careful."

"That's the plan," he mumbled, and he headed in the direction of the fallen gunman.

He kept watch on Eve and tried to push aside all the other things that crept into his mind, but Grayson knew once this threat was over, he had a dozen other things to deal with—especially Eve.

Grayson reached the spot he'd last seen the gunman, and he cursed. The gunman was still there, in the exact place where he'd taken his last breath. His gun had dropped from his hand.

"He's dead," Grayson relayed to Eve.

She started toward him, practically running. "You're sure?"

Grayson leaned down and checked for a pulse, but that was just to keep everything straight for the reports he'd have to write up later. "Yeah."

Eve was nearly out of breath by the time she made it to him. She took one look at the man's ash-white face, and she shivered and leaned against Grayson.

He'd seen death before, maybe Eve had, too, but it was different seeing it like this. She was trembling hard now, and there were tears in her eyes, so he took her arm and led her away. There was no need for her to see any more of this.

"Why did he try to kill us?" she whispered, her voice clogged with emotion.

Grayson didn't know for sure, but he figured it had something to do with the dead woman in the photos. Maybe this gunman had killed her. "I'll find out," he promised Eve.

Since she looked ready to collapse, Grayson pulled her into his arms. She didn't put up a fight, probably because there was no fight left in her. This had taken, and would continue to take, a lot out of her. Grayson regretted that, but he didn't regret that this guy was dead.

Or that he was able to give some small comfort to Eve.

She was still trembling, but her breathing started to level. What she didn't do was move away, and Grayson was thankful for it. He hated to admit it, but the shooting had shaken him, and being this close to Eve was giving him as much comfort as he was hopefully giving her.

Even now, under the worst of circumstances, he couldn't help but notice how nicely Eve still fit in his arms. Her body practically molded against his.

"We're not bad people," she mumbled. "This shouldn't happen to us."

Yeah. But Grayson knew that neither good nor bad had anything to do with this. The dead man was likely trying to cover up a murder, and in his experience people would do anything and everything to avoid jail.

She pulled back and stared up at him. Their gazes connected, and that *fit,* too. He could read her so well and knew the tears were about to spill again. She had a good reason to cry, and later he would lend her his shoulder, but for now, he had things to do.

"This guy might not be the one who killed Nina Manning. He could be just a trigger-man," Grayson explained, trying to keep his voice void of emotion so that she would stay calm.

He failed.

Despite her leveled breathing, Eve still looked anything but calm. So, to soothe himself and her, he brushed a kiss on her temple and then eased back so that she was no longer in his embrace.

"The only way we make this better," Grayson whispered to her, "is to end it. I have to find out why this man came after us."

Eve's bottom lip trembled, and she nodded. Seconds later, she nodded again. "I'm not weak," she assured him. Something he already knew.

"You just saw me kill a man. There's nothing weak about your reaction. Truth is, I'm shaking inside." And that was the truth. Killing didn't come easy to him, and he hoped like hell that it never did.

Another nod. Eve blinked back tears and reached out to him, but neither of her hands was free. She had her gun in her right hand. The cell phone in the other.

He took the cell from her and motioned for her to move even farther away from the body. "I'll call Dade," he let her know. And he tried. But the signal was so low that the call wouldn't go through. Grayson sent him a text instead and gave Dade their location.

Eve slipped her gun into her pocket and pulled her coat tightly against her. It wasn't freezing, but it wasn't warm, either. Besides, she was battling adrenaline and nerves, and that was no doubt contributing to the trembling.

"What now?" she asked.

Grayson took a deep breath before he answered. "We wait."

She blinked. "For how long?"

He heard the unasked questions, and he knew she wouldn't like the answers to any of them. "The text will eventually get through to Dade, and he'll come after us."

"Good." Her face relaxed a little. "Then we should walk back to the road to meet him."

Grayson glanced back at the body. "The

coyotes won't leave a fresh kill alone for long. I need to preserve the crime scene as much as possible because I need an ID on this guy."

Eve started shaking her head. "But I need to get to Austin."

He nodded and settled for saying, "I know."

"No. You don't know." She huffed and blinked back more tears.

Hell.

Well, at least she wasn't shaking so hard, but this was about to get ugly.

"You don't know," she repeated, and she just kept on repeating it until the words and the tears got the best of her. She sagged against a tree.

"Eve," he said reaching out to her, but she just moved away.

Her breath broke on a sob. "I've made some terrible mistakes in my life. First, giving you that ultimatum. And then I promised my heart and life to a man I didn't love. I'm the Typhoid Mary of relationships, Grayson, but I know I'm meant to be a mother."

She was. Grayson didn't doubt that. Heck, she'd practically been a mother to his youngest brother. Grayson, however, didn't have a good track record. And he tried one last time to convince Eve of that.

"I'm not the man you want to father your baby," he insisted.

She opened her mouth to say something, but Grayson didn't want her to tell him something along the lines of his being the only man she wanted for that job. He couldn't hear that. Not now. Not with Eve falling apart like this.

"I sucked as a father," he continued, trying to snag her gaze. Eye contact might help her see the determination. "My brother Gage is dead."

"Gage died doing a job he loved," she clarified. "You couldn't and wouldn't have stopped him from joining the Justice Department any more than he could have stopped you from being sheriff of Silver Creek."

Maybe. But that didn't change things. Besides, Gage was just one of his failures.

"Dade has got so much rage inside him. Nate's just one bad day away from needing professional help. And Mason? Hell, I wouldn't be surprised if he hunted our father down just so he could kill him in cold blood." Grayson paused because he had to. "That's the kind of family I raised."

Now she made eye contact, and the jolt was like a head-on collision. Grayson had hoped she would see his emotion, and maybe she did, but he saw hers in complete vivid detail. The pain. The need.

The hopelessness of her situation.

"If I helped you," he managed to say, "I'd just screw things up again."

She swiped away the tears and stared at him. "If you don't help me, I'll never know what it's like to be a mother. I'll never have a part of my life that I want more than my next breath." She walked closer. "Grayson, you would have no responsibility in this, other than having sex with me. I swear, *no responsibility.*"

He had to say no. Had to. And Grayson just kept repeating that.

But he knew the reality here.

Even if Dade got the text and responded right away, it would be an hour or more before they could get this body out of the woods. Grayson would need another vehicle since his truck was in the creek. It would be nightfall or later before he could get Eve to a clinic in Austin. Since it was just three days before Christmas, it was likely the clinics had already closed for the day. Maybe for the rest of the holiday week.

Still, Grayson had to say no.

Didn't he?

"Don't think too much," she whispered, walking closer.

The cold air mixed with her breath and created a misty fog around her face. It seemed unreal. Like a dream. And Grayson had had so many dreams about her that he nearly got lost in the moment.

Oh, man.

She could still make him burn.

Eve stopped, directly in front of him. So close he could take in her scent. She leaned in and put her mouth to his ear. She didn't touch him. Didn't have to touch him. Her scent was enough. He fought to hang on to the denial he intended to give her, but it was a battle that Grayson knew he was losing.

Worse, he *wanted* to lose.

"Just consider this a big favor for an old friend," she whispered.

A friend? Eve was plenty of things, but she wasn't a friend. Whatever she was, she was pulling him closer. And closer.

"Please," she said. Just that one word. Her warm breath brushed against his mouth like a kiss.

He looked into her eyes and didn't look beyond that. Yeah. He could say no. He could turn and walk away.

But that wasn't what Grayson was going to do.

What he did was exactly as Eve had said.

He didn't think too much. He didn't look beyond this moment and the bad mistake he was about to make.

Grayson cursed and pulled her to him.

Chapter 8

Eve was too afraid to ask Grayson if he was sure about this. She was too afraid to delay even a second because she couldn't risk that he would change his mind.

This had to happen, and it had to happen now.

Grayson was obviously with her on the *now* part. He slid down, his back against the tree, and he pulled her down with him.

Eve's breath was racing already. Her heart pounded against her ribs so hard that it felt her bones would break. She was trembling, scared and cold, but she pushed all those uncomfortable things aside and pressed her mouth to his.

Big mistake.

She felt him stiffen, and the air between them changed. He'd agreed to the sex, to the making a baby part, but that stiff mouth told her that he wasn't ready or willing to go back to where they'd been.

"All right," she mumbled, hoping the sound of her own voice would steady her nerves.

It didn't, but Eve didn't let raw nerves or Grayson's steely look get to her. She worked fast, sliding up her dress and moving onto his lap in the same motion. She didn't meet his gaze. Didn't want to. This was already difficult enough without seeing the proof of what he was thinking.

And he was no doubt thinking this was a big mistake.

Eve didn't let him voice that. She knew what she had to do. She'd had years of experience making out with Grayson. After all, they'd had their first kiss when she was fifteen, and they had spent years driving each other crazy.

She knew how to make him crazy.

Eve didn't kiss him again, but she put her mouth right next to his ear. He liked the breath and heat. He liked the pressure and the touch of her tongue there. Well, at least that's what used to fire him up. She had another moment of panic when she realized that her mouth might not have the same effect on him as it had back then. He might push her—

Grayson made a slight, familiar sound.

If she'd been any other woman, she might not have even heard the catch in his chest, the small burst of breath that he tried to choke back. But Eve heard those things, and she knew exactly what they meant. This was still a fire spot for him. So were her hands on his chest. Since his shirt was already partially unbuttoned, she ran her fingers through his chest hair. And lower.

Grayson liked lower.

Still did, apparently.

Because by the time she trailed her fingers from his stomach and to the front of his jeans, she found him already huge and hard. She pressed her sex against his.

Eve suddenly didn't feel so cold.

A thought flashed through her head—this was like riding a bicycle. Well, better actually. Her body knew exactly what Grayson could do to her, how he could make her soar. And fall. That wouldn't happen now. It couldn't. She had to keep this as clinical as possible. He was merely a sperm donor here and not her lover.

Eve fumbled with his zipper and finally managed to lower it. No thanks to her hands. She was trembling. So was her mouth, but that didn't seem to affect the kisses she lowered to his neck.

She reached to take off her panties, but Grayson latched on to her hand. His grip was as hard as the part of him she was pressed against.

Her gaze snapped to his, and again Eve was terrified that he was stopping this. But Grayson didn't look her in the eyes. He made another of those sounds, a growl from deep within his throat, and he grabbed her with his other hand. He turned her, shoving her back against the tree. The impact and her surprise nearly knocked the breath out of her.

Grayson seemed to have no trouble breathing. He yanked off her panties and pushed his hips between her legs. He was on his knees now, and the weight of him pinned her to the tree.

For just a moment, she registered the rough bark against her back and bottom. His raw grip. The harsh profanity he was mumbling. Then, he thrust into her. One long stroke that was nearly as rough as the hold he had on her wrists.

Her body gave way to his sex. Welcoming him. Yes, he was rough, and the thrusts inside her didn't become gentle, either. Of course, he knew her body as well as she knew his. And

Grayson knew her. Gentle didn't work for *her*. She had always been in such a hurry to have him that she had begged for hard and fast.

Exactly what he was giving her now.

The man knew what he was doing, that was for sure. He'd learned to make love with her. He knew how to bring her to climax within seconds. Normally, Eve would have gladly surrendered to that climax. She would have surrendered to Grayson, but she instinctively knew that would make the aftermath even worse than it already would be.

And it would be *bad*.

This would cut her off from Grayson forever. Once he'd had time to apply his logical no-shades-of-gray mind to this, he would feel that she'd manipulated him. And she had. Later, Eve would deal with it, too. But for now, she pressed her mouth to the spot just below his ear. She whispered his name.

"Grayson."

The trigger, he had once called it. To finish him off, all she had to do was say his name. It had just the effect she knew it would.

He thrust into her one last time and said her name, too. *Almost.*

"Damn you, Eve," Grayson cursed.

And he finished what he'd started.

Chapter 9

Grayson got up as soon as he could move. He fixed his clothes and then put some distance between Eve and him. He couldn't go far, but even a few yards would help.

He hoped.

Behind him, he could hear Eve milling around. She was also mumbling. Grayson didn't want to figure out what she was saying. He didn't want to figure out anything except why he'd snapped and done the very thing he'd sworn he wouldn't do.

"If you're waiting for me to say I'm sorry, then you'll be waiting a long time," Eve let him know. "Because I'm not sorry, and I hope you're not, either."

Oh, he was. Sorry and stupid. But that wouldn't change what had happened. There was no way he could justify having sex with Eve. Yes, she might get pregnant. She might finally get that baby she wanted, but that put him right in a position he didn't want to be.

He didn't want to be a father.

Of course, the odds were against Eve having conceived. Grayson had no idea of the stats, but even with her at the prime time of the month, this had to be a long shot.

Hell.

That bothered him, too.

He wanted Eve to have this chance at motherhood, but Grayson wanted what he wanted, as well. Too bad he couldn't quite put a finger on what he did want. Nor did he have time to figure it out. His phone beeped, and he glanced down at the message as it came onto the screen.

"Is it Dade?" Eve asked, hurrying to his side. She was still fixing her clothes, and she smelled like sex. Looked like it, too, Grayson noticed when he risked glancing at her. He looked away as fast as he could.

"Yeah." Grayson worked his way through the abbreviations Dade had used in the message and gave her a summary. "He used my cell phone to pinpoint our location and will be here soon."

She made a sound of relief. So different from the sound she'd made just minutes ago when he'd taken her against the tree. The memory of it flashed through his head, and Grayson knew that memory would give him no peace.

His phone beeped again, and there was a new message from Dade. "He wants me to take a picture of the body," Grayson relayed to Eve. "As soon as we have a better signal, I can send it to the Rangers and they can feed it through the facial recognition program."

Something that Grayson should have already thought of, but then he'd had sex with Eve on his mind.

He cursed himself again.

"Wait here," he ordered, and Grayson walked across the woods to the body. Even the mini break from Eve might help because right now his stomach was knotted even harder than it had been in the middle of the attack.

The dead man was still there, of course, sprawled out among the clumps of dried leaves and fallen tree limbs. Grayson snapped a couple of pictures and checked the signal. Still too weak to send the photos, but he made a mental note to keep checking. He made another mental note not to do any more looking at Eve. No thinking about Eve. No more need for her that was generated below the belt.

Hard to do with her standing there in that body-hugging dress.

"Thank you," she whispered when he went back to her.

He didn't want to hear this. "Don't," Grayson warned. "Don't say anything." He wasn't a man who dwelled on regrets, but by God he could make an exception.

She stepped in front of him and forced eye contact. "Thank you," Eve repeated, and she leaned in pressed a chaste kiss on his cheek.

His cheek!

Here his body was still burning for her, and she had risked giving him a brotherly kiss like that. The woman really was playing with fire.

Grayson stepped back and fastened his attention on the area where the dead man was. "Did I hurt you?" he growled.

"No." Eve answered it so quickly that she'd probably anticipated the question. Which meant he'd been too rough. Grayson shot her an over-the-shoulder glance to let her know that.

She shrugged. "I don't mind a little rough. But you're aware of that."

Yeah, he was. He knew every inch of her

body and could have gotten her off with just a touch. But Grayson had tried to keep the pleasure factor out of this. For him that was impossible. His body was humming, and well satisfied, even though his brain was confused as hell.

"How long before you know if this worked?" he asked.

"I'm not sure. I'll have to ask my doctor." She hesitated. "I figured I wouldn't call you or anything with the results. I thought it would be easier that way. Is that okay?"

Was it? Grayson didn't have a clue what was okay. His brain was a mess right now. "Yeah," he settled for saying.

She pulled her coat around her and shivered. Eve was obviously cold, but Grayson intended to do nothing about that. He'd already done enough for the day.

"I don't want you to tell your family about this," she insisted. "As soon as we're out of here, I'll leave so you won't have to see me."

He gave her another look that was probably more scowl than anything else.

She huffed. "Grayson, I'm not stupid. I know what's going on in your head, and you'll want to put as much distance between us as possible."

True. But distance was going to be a problem until he figured out why the man had wanted her dead. Grayson was about to remind her of that when he heard Dade call out to them.

"Over here!" Grayson answered. With Eve right behind him, he went in the direction of his brother's voice.

Eve raked her hand through her hair, trying to fix it, and she brushed off the bits of leaves and twigs from her coat. Grayson tried to do the same.

He soon spotted Dade, and he wasn't alone. Deputy Melissa Garza was with him. Mel, as she liked to be called. And Grayson was thankful Dade had brought her along.

"You okay?" Dade asked when he was still a good twenty yards away.

Grayson nodded, but he was far from okay. He tipped his head to the body. "Single gunshot wound to the chest, and he bled out. It's the man we chased into the woods behind Eve's cottage."

Mel began to trudge her way through to the dead man, but Dade stayed on the path that led directly toward Grayson. As his brother walked closer, he glanced at both Eve and him. Not an ordinary glance but a suspicious one.

"I have the photos," Grayson said showing Dade his cell. Best to get Dade's suspicious mind back where it belonged—on the investigation. "Is the medical examiner on the way?"

"Yeah. He and his crew are right behind us." Dade volleyed more glances between the two of them.

"Good. Mel can stay with the body, and you can get Eve and me out of here," Grayson instructed. "I want to get the photos to the Rangers."

Dade called out Grayson's instructions to Mel, and the deputy nodded.

"Are you really okay?" Dade asked Eve as the three of them headed back toward the road.

"You mean other than the raw nerves, the tear-stained cheeks and adrenaline crash?" The corner of her mouth lifted. "Yes, I'm okay."

Dade hooked his arm around her shoulders. "I wish you could have had a better homecoming." He shifted his attention to Grayson but didn't say anything. Dade's left eyebrow lifted.

Grayson ignored him and kept on walking. Thankfully, they soon reached a spot where the cell signal was stronger, and he fired off the photos. If the dead man had a police record, then it wouldn't take the Rangers long to come up with an ID.

It took a good ten minutes for them to get back to the road where Dade had a cruiser waiting. Dade helped Eve into the front passenger's seat, closed the door and turned back around to stare at Grayson.

"Don't ask," Grayson growled in a whisper.

Dade lifted his shoulder. "Hey, you got my vote if you're getting back together with Eve."

"It's not a vote." Grayson cursed. "And what part of 'don't ask' didn't you understand?"

"The *don't* part." Dade smirked as only a younger brother could manage to do.

Grayson cursed some more. "Look, I'm in a bad mood. The kind of mood where I'd love to beat someone senseless. My advice? Stay out of my way, or that someone will be you." He threw open the door and climbed into the driver's seat.

As soon as Dade got in, Grayson sped back toward town. His mood improved a little when he saw the ME's van approaching from the opposite direction. That meant Mel wouldn't have to stay out there very long, and that was good. He needed all his deputies back at the station so he could figure out what the heck was going on.

"Any idea how the dead man tracked you down?" Dade asked from the backseat.

Grayson was about to say no, but then he groaned. "Probably a tracking device. He put one on Eve's car, we know that, and I'm guessing he put one on the truck, too."

Eve made a small gasping sound of surprise.

"I'll have someone check when they fish your truck from the creek," Dade assured him. But Grayson heard the hesitation in his brother's voice. Dade was no doubt wondering why Grayson hadn't thought of the possibility of a tracking device before he'd driven the truck away from his office.

Grayson didn't need another reason to put some distance between Eve and him, but there it was. He was thinking like a rookie, and the stakes were too high for him to make another mistake.

This mistake could have gotten Eve killed.

He wouldn't forget that.

Since Eve was shivering, Grayson decided to turn up the heat, though the adrenaline was probably more responsible than the chilly temperature. Eve apparently had the same idea because she reached at the same time he did. Their hands collided. And she pulled back as if he'd scalded her. Ironic, since just a half hour earlier he'd been deep inside her. Still, it was good they were in agreement about this no-touching thing.

"Uh, I'm guessing Eve's in protective custody?" Dade wanted to know. It sounded like a loaded question.

Eve turned in the seat to look at Dade, and Grayson nodded. "She can stay at the ranch."

"At the ranch?" She shook her head. "That's probably not a good idea."

Yeah. He was in agreement with that, too. The sex against the tree had only created more tension and friction between them, but there couldn't be any more mistakes.

"You might not have to be there long," Grayson explained. "We just need to tie up some loose ends on this case." He looked in the rearview mirror so he could see Dade. "Any more news on our DB, Nina Manning?"

"Still waiting on the preliminaries. Once we have the next of kin identified, we can talk to them, as well."

Grayson shook his head. "You said there was a missing person's report filed on her a year ago. Who filed that?"

"Her mother, Theresa Manning. She was a single parent, no record of the father, and Theresa died about a month ago. Yeah," Dade added when Grayson glanced at him in the mirror. "Theresa was diabetic and died from an insulin overdose. Could have been an accident, but I asked the Houston cops to look into it."

Yes, because the timing was suspicious.

Grayson's phone buzzed, and he saw the caller was from the Texas Ranger lab. "Sheriff Ryland," he answered and put the call on speaker so Dade could hear.

"Ranger Egan Caldwell," the man identified himself. "I have a match on the photos of the dead man."

Grayson released the breath he'd been holding. "Who is he?"

"Leon Ames. He has a record, obviously. Seven years ago for assault with a deadly weapon. He spent two years in a Bexar county jail and is still on probation."

Well, prison hadn't rehabilitated him, that's for sure. "He tried to kill me twice today, and he's in the photograph with the dead woman, Nina Manning. Is there a connection?"

"Nothing obvious, but he's got a history with the other man in the photo, Sebastian Collier."

"How?" Dade and Grayson asked in unison. Eve leaned closer to the phone and listened.

"Leon Ames works…worked for Sebastian's father, Claude. He was a handyman at their San Antonio estate."

Handyman. That was an interesting word, considering the photograph with the dead woman and the attempts to kill Eve and him.

"I'm faxing you the rest of the report," the ranger continued. "For what it's worth, I don't think Leon Ames was working alone. From everything I can see, he was nothing more than a lackey."

"What makes you think that?" Grayson asked.

"A large sum of money deposited into his bank account the day after the murder. Twenty thousand dollars. We can't trace the money because he made the deposit in cash. My guess is that money was a payoff for services rendered."

Grayson suspected as much. "So, who hired Leon—Claude or Sebastian?"

"Either is possible," the ranger answered. "But I think all roads in this investigation lead to the Colliers, and that you'll find a killer at the estate."

Chapter 10

Eve needed a friendly face, and she saw one the moment Grayson pulled to a stop in front of the Collier estate. His brother, Lieutenant Nate Ryland, was there waiting for them on the sidewalk in front of the towering black-iron fence that fronted the equally towering Collier estate.

Nate smiled, his dimples flashing, and the moment she stepped from the car, he pulled her into his arms. "Even under these circumstances, it's good to see you," Nate whispered.

"It's good to see you, too." And Eve meant it. She'd never felt more at home than in the arms of a Ryland, and Nate was no exception.

She inched back to meet his gaze and return the smile. The Ryland DNA was there all right, etched over his perfectly chiseled face, black hair and storm-gray eyes. But Nate was smooth around the cowboy-edges in his dark blue suit, which was a job requirement for San Antonio P.D. Like the rest of the Ryland clan, he was more at home in Wranglers and on the back of a horse.

Would her baby be the same?

Her baby, she mentally repeated. And she felt her smile deepen. Yes, a pregnancy was a long shot, but it was possible that she was well on her way to getting the child she'd always wanted.

"Eve?" Nate said, drawing her out of her daydream. "You okay?"

"Of course. I was just distracted for a moment." Eve stared at him, and her smile faded when she remembered what Nate had gone through. "I'm sorry about your wife's death," she whispered.

Eve was even sorrier that she hadn't gone to the funeral or spoken to him about it before now. Nate had always felt like a brother to her, and she'd let him down at a time when he no doubt needed all of his friends. "How are you handling things?"

His smile faded, too. "It's, uh, complicated," he mumbled. Nate's gaze swung in Grayson's direction, an indication to her that this conversation was over. "Are you ready to do battle with the Colliers?"

"Considering their hired gun tried to kill us, yeah, I'm ready."

Nate gave a crisp nod. As a lieutenant, he'd no doubt done his share of interrogations. He was also a cop with some clout when it came to handling an investigation.

And Grayson.

If Nate hadn't had some influence, Eve wouldn't have been allowed to tag along. As it was, she'd practically had to beg Grayson to let her come. He'd wanted to tuck her safely away at the ranch. Eve wanted to be safe, but she didn't want that at the expense of learning the truth. She had taken the incriminating photo, and she wanted to confront the person responsible for what was going on.

"Anything I should know before we go inside?" Grayson asked his brother.

"Well, they haven't lawyered up. But I doubt that means you'll get a lot of cooperation, especially when you link the dead woman to their now dead employee."

Eve hoped Nate was wrong. She wanted answers today so she could start distancing herself from Grayson. She couldn't keep leaning on these Ryland shoulders.

"So, Claude and Sebastian know that Leon was killed?" she clarified.

"They do. And when I spoke to them over the phone, I also told them that Leon tried to murder both of you." Nate walked toward the gate and flashed his badge at the monitor. Seconds later, the gate creaked open.

"I'd like to handle the interview myself," Grayson insisted.

"Figured you would. But if we learn anything we can use to hold either one of them, I need to make the arrest since we're not sure where this murder occurred."

An arrest. Eve hoped that would happen, and then things could finally get back to normal. Well, maybe. If she was indeed pregnant, then nothing would be *normal* again.

Nate shot her a glance. "And I hoped you would say as little as possible. I want them to see you, so they'll know that the picture you took is no longer a reason to come after you. That's the only reason I'm allowing you in the middle of a murder investigation."

She nodded, mumbled a thanks.

"Eve knows the rules," Grayson said, and it sounded like a warning. He walked ahead of them toward the porch that stretched the entire width of the three-story house. There were dozens of white columns, each of them ringed with fresh holly, and a five-foot-tall vertical wreath hung on the door.

Nate fell in step alongside her. "Did something happen between you two?" he asked.

What—did she have a big sign stuck to her back proclaiming that she'd had sex with Grayson? Of course, *sex* was a very loose term for what had happened between them. It had seemed more like a biology experiment.

And that, she reminded herself, was exactly what she'd asked of Grayson.

No strings attached. No emotion. No discussion.

Well, she'd gotten all of that. He had hardly said two words to her when they'd gone back to the sheriff's office to change his clothes. Or on the drive from Silver Creek to her San Antonio condo so she could get a change of clothes, as well. Ditto for more of his silence on the drive to the Collier estate.

And that was just as well.

He was making it easier for her to walk away.

"Nothing happened," she lied.

Nate made a sound that could have meant anything and joined Grayson on the porch as he rang the doorbell. Eve stayed just behind them. A maid wearing a uniform opened the door, and without saying a word, she ushered them through the marble-floored foyer and into a sitting room where two men waited for them.

The room was decorated in varying shades of white and cream. A stark contrast to the floor-to-ceiling Christmas tree that was practically smothered in shiny blood-red ornaments. After the real blood she'd seen today, the sight of those ornaments twisted her stomach a little.

Eve recognized both men in the room—Claude from his photos in the newspapers and Sebastian from the picture she'd taken of him at the rodeo. Both men were dressed in suits. Claude's was black. His son's, a dark gray. Both men were sipping something from cut-crystal glasses that looked and smelled expensive.

"Sheriff Grayson Ryland," he said, stepping ahead of Nate and her. "This is my brother, Lt. Nate Ryland from SAPD, and Eve Warren."

"Ah, Ms. Warren, the woman who took the photo in question," Sebastian quickly supplied. He crossed the room and shook all of their hands. His expression and greeting were friendly enough, but Eve wondered just how long that would last.

The friendly demeanor didn't extend to the other Collier in the room. Claude was a carbon copy of his son, but he was at least twenty pounds thinner and his scowl bunched up his otherwise classic features. His navy blue eyes were narrowed, and he watched them as if they were thieves about to run off with the family silver. He also didn't ask them to sit, probably because he hoped this would be a short visit. Or maybe he was just naturally rude.

"Yes, I took the picture," Eve answered when Sebastian continued to stare at her. "How did you know about that?"

That question earned her scolding looks from Nate and Grayson, who obviously didn't want her involved in this questioning, but Sebastian only flashed that thousand-watt smile. A smile that probably worked wonders on his business associates, but to her it felt slimy.

Just like the man himself.

"A journalist friend told me," Sebastian volunteered. "I understand it was going to be printed in tomorrow's newspaper. But then you managed to ID the unfortunate victim."

"Yes," Grayson verified. He kept his gaze pinned to Sebastian. "Mind explaining what you and your *handyman* were doing in the photo with Nina Manning?"

Sebastian opened his mouth to answer, but his father's voice boomed through the room.

"Leon Ames is not my handyman. I fired him three days ago."

Grayson and Nate exchanged glances. "Why?" Grayson demanded.

Claude shrugged as if the answer wasn't important. He responded only after Grayson continued to stare at him. "Erratic behavior," Claude finally supplied. The man couldn't have sounded snootier if he'd tried. "I expect impeccable behavior from my employees, and Leon didn't live up to that."

"How so?" Grayson pressed.

Claude blew out an irritated breath. "If you must know, he used one of the family cars to run a personal errand. I questioned him, he lied about it and I dismissed him. End of story."

Grayson matched the irritated breath response. "No. It's not the end of it. Because the day before you fired him, Leon and your son were photographed with a woman who was murdered."

"I can explain that," Sebastian offered, still sounding very cooperative. "I went to the charity rodeo, and I ran into Leon and the woman. I believe they were lovers."

"Lovers?" Grayson again. "Leon was twice her age."

Claude flexed his eyebrows. "Then, maybe

lover isn't the right term. I think the woman was a pro. She was hitting up Leon for cash."

Since Nina did indeed have a record for prostitution, that could be true, but Eve wasn't about to believe him. Sebastian almost certainly wouldn't admit if he'd been the one who hired Nina for her *services*.

"Tell me everything you remember about the meeting," Grayson demanded, looking directly at Sebastian.

Sebastian took a sip of his drink and gave another nonchalant lift of his shoulder. "As I said, I went to the charity rodeo so I could make a donation and ran into Leon. The woman was with him, and they seemed to be, well, cozy."

"In the picture they appeared to be angry," Grayson fired back.

"That came later." Sebastian didn't hesitate. "The woman's attitude became less friendly when Leon refused to give her money."

Grayson stepped closer to Sebastian. "Did she say what the money was for?"

Sebastian shook his head. "I didn't listen to their conversation, Sheriff. The woman was obviously low-rent. Probably high on drugs. Once I realized that, I moved away and let them finish their discussion. I didn't want to be seen in that kind of company."

"Did it seem as if Leon knew Nina before this meeting?" Nate asked.

"I'm not sure." Sebastian finished his drink in one gulp.

"You should be talking to Leon's friends about that," Claude interrupted. "I won't have my family's good name dragged through the mud for the likes of Leon Ames."

Grayson gave him a flat look. "I don't suppose you have the names of Leon's friends?"

Claude's mouth twisted as if he'd tasted something bitter. "I do not make it a habit of delving into the personal lives of my employees." He slapped his glass onto the table. "And that's the end of this interview. Anything else goes through our family attorneys."

Sebastian gave an embarrassed smile. "I've already told you everything I know."

"Not quite." Despite Claude's rude dismissal, Grayson stayed put. "When's the last time you saw Leon and the dead woman?"

"Probably just a few minutes after Miss Warren here snapped the photo. I left, and I have no idea where they went." Sebastian checked his watch. "Now, if you'll excuse me, I need to get ready for our guests. We're having a small Christmas gathering here tonight."

"If you remember anything else about the encounter with Nina and Leon," Grayson said to Sebastian, "I want you to call me." He extracted a business card from his jacket pocket and dropped it on the glass end table. "I'll also need you to go to SAPD and give a written statement."

Sebastian groaned softly. "Please tell me that can wait until after the holidays. Christmas is only three days away."

"And SAPD will be open all day," Grayson fired back. "A woman is dead, and she deserves justice. I need that statement and anything else you can remember about Leon's friends."

"Of course," Sebastian finally agreed, but he was no longer so cordial. His mouth tightened.

Both father and son turned to walk out, but they stopped when the sound of a woman's high heels echoed through the room. They all turned in the direction of the sound, and Eve spotted a curvy blonde in a plunging liquid-silver dress, who was making her way toward them. She, too, had a drink in a crystal highball glass, and she was teetering on five-inch red heels that were the exact color of the Christmas ornaments.

"Claude, you didn't tell me that we had guests." She clucked her tongue and smiled first at Grayson. Then Nate. She didn't even spare Eve a glance.

"They're not guests," Claude snapped. "They're cops. And they were just leaving."

"Leaving?" The woman gave a quick fake pout. "Well, let me introduce myself. I'm Annabel Collier, Claude's wife." Her cherry-lacquered smile went south when she glanced at Sebastian. "And I'm his stepmother."

Eve hadn't studied the background info on Annabel, but she was betting that stepmother and son were close to the same age. Annabel was clearly a trophy wife.

A drunk one.

"The maid was about to show them out," Claude reiterated, and just like that, the maid appeared in the doorway of the sitting room.

"I can do that," Annabel volunteered. She hooked her arm through Grayson's, and Eve didn't think it was her imagination that the woman pressed the side of her double Ds against Grayson's chest.

"Isn't the estate beautiful this time of year?" Annabel babbled on. Some of her drink sloshed onto the floor and the toes of those red stilettos. "I love all the sparkles and the presents. Claude is very generous with presents, you know. I peeked, and all I can say is five carats, platinum setting." She punctuated that with a drunken giggle.

Behind them, Eve heard Claude mumble something, but both Sebastian and he stayed put as Annabel escorted Grayson to the door. Nate and Eve followed, and Eve wondered if she could trip the bimbo who was hanging all over Grayson. Since Grayson and she weren't together, it didn't make sense to be jealous, but Eve felt it anyway.

Annabel threw open the door, and the cold December wind poured into the foyer and rustled the shimmering gold wreath. Despite her strapless dress she stepped onto the porch with them. She glanced over her shoulder, and when her gaze returned to them, she was a changed woman. No bimbo smile, and her sapphire-blue eyes were suddenly intense.

Eve was too dumbfounded to do anything but watch, which was probably a good thing.

Annabel plucked something from her cleavage and pressed it into Grayson's hand, which she pretended to shake. "The Colliers have secrets," she whispered, her bottom lip trembling. "Deadly ones."

Annabel giggled again, sliding right back into the persona of the drunken trophy wife. "Happy holidays," she told them as she stepped back inside. She gave Grayson one last pleading look, and then shut the door.

"What was that all about?" Nate mumbled.

But Grayson didn't answer. He hurried off the porch and toward the car. So did Nate and Eve. He waited until they were outside the gates and away from the security cameras that dotted the fence.

Then Grayson opened his hand so that Nate and Eve could see what Annabel had given him.

Eve stared it and shook her head.

What the heck was going on, and why had Annabel given them *this*?

Chapter 11

Grayson was several steps beyond exhaustion, but he kept his eyes on the road. It was nearly dark, and the temperature had dropped, and the last thing he needed was to wreck another car today.

"Anything?" he asked Eve again.

It was a question he'd asked her several times since they'd left San Antonio nearly a half hour earlier. Most of that time, Eve had been using the laptop that she'd picked up from her condo so she could view the pictures.

Pictures on the tiny memory card that Annabel had given them.

Grayson had already emailed a copy of the card's contents to the crime lab in Austin, but he wanted to have a closer look for himself as to what Annabel had considered important enough to pass along to a sheriff who was investigating her husband and stepson.

Eve shifted the laptop to a position so that Grayson could see. He glanced at the screen and saw the thumbnails of the photographs. There were dozens of them.

"Annabel obviously likes to take pictures, but I think I finally have them sorted," Eve mumbled. She tapped the ones in the first row. "These are shots taken in what appears to be Claude's office. My guess is Annabel took them with a hidden camera mounted somewhere in the room because the angle never changes."

"Anything incriminating?" Grayson asked.

"Hard to tell. Claude's obviously having a discussion with this dark-haired woman, but there's nothing sexual going on. I think they're arguing."

Grayson agreed. Everything about their body language conveyed anger, not romance. "I need to find out who that woman is." And the crime lab could maybe help with that.

"Well, I think we can rule her out as a mistress. Claude seems to prefer women half his age, and this woman looks to be about fifty."

Eve enlarged the photos on the next row, and she made a sound of surprise.

"What?" Grayson asked. He didn't want to fully take his eyes off the road, but Eve's reaction grabbed his attention.

"There are a dozen or more shots taken in a hotel lobby. An expensive hotel, judging from the decor. And there's Nina." She pointed to the next series of pictures. "Nina's not alone, either. Both Claude and Sebastian are there with her."

Eve met his gaze. "That means Sebastian lied about never having seen Nina."

Yeah. Annabel had been right about family secrets. Was this what she'd meant?

"Is a lie enough to arrest Sebastian?" Eve asked.

"No. With his money and connections, we need more. We need a motive." Grayson turned off the highway and onto the ranch road that would take him home.

She huffed and pushed her hair from her face. Eve was obviously exhausted, too. Even with the watery light from the laptop screen, he could see the dark circles beneath her eyes. He could also see how damn attractive she was, and he wondered if there was ever a time he wouldn't look at her and think just that.

"Maybe Sebastian and Nina were lovers?"

Eve tossed out there. She was obviously un-
aware that he was sneaking glimpses of not
just the photographs but of her. "Maybe Sebastian snapped when he found out his lover
also had a romantic interest in his father?"

Grayson shook his head. "That doesn't look
like a lover's encounter. Even though it's possible that one or both had sex with her, and
Nina was trying to blackmail them. After all,
Claude did say he wouldn't have his family's
good name dragged through the mud. Maybe
this was his way of making sure that didn't
happen."

And Claude could have hired Leon to kill
a blackmailing Nina.

But then why was Sebastian in the picture?

Better yet, why had Annabel given him this
incriminating evidence?

Grayson wasn't sure, but he intended to find
out. He'd already requested a more detailed
background check on Nina and all the Colliers, including Annabel.

"There are some pictures taken at the charity rodeo," Eve let him know. "Not mine.
These are ones that Annabel or someone else
shot. High angle, zoom lens. She was probably
in the top seats of the stadium."

Maybe so that the men wouldn't notice her,
which meant that Annabel probably knew she

was snapping pictures of something incriminating.

"Did she photograph the encounter with Leon, Nina and Sebastian?" Grayson asked.

He took the last turn to the ranch and could see the lights of the sprawling two-story house just ahead. Sometimes, he took home for granted. But not tonight. It was a welcome sight.

"Not that I can readily see," Eve answered, her attention still nailed to the computer screen. "I need to enlarge the photos and study them."

"Later." The pictures were important, perhaps even critical, but he wanted to get her settled into the guestroom first. He'd already called the housekeeper, Bessie Watkins, to let her know they were on the way so that she could prepare the guestroom.

Eve looked up as if surprised to see they were already at the ranch. "Wow," she mumbled.

That reaction was no doubt for the Christmas lights. There were hundreds of them lining the fence that led all the way to the main house. Even the shrubs had been decked with twinkling lights, and there were two fully decorated Christmas trees on each end of the porch.

"Bessie did this," Grayson explained. "For Nate's daughter, Kimmie. It's her first Christmas."

Grayson felt a tightness in his chest. Because it was a Christmas that his niece wouldn't be able to spend with her mother. It made him even more determined to keep Eve safe. And he'd taken measures to make sure that happened.

The ranch was huge, over three thousand acres, but it was equipped with a full security system that monitored all parts of the house and property. There were also at least a dozen ranch hands in quarters on the grounds.

Then, there were his brothers.

Mason and Dade were still at work in town, but soon they would return for the night. Nate, too, even though Kimmie and he lived in a separate wing of the ranch house. The youngest, Kade, was at his apartment in Austin where he worked for the FBI, but he could be at the ranch in an hour if necessary.

Grayson hoped it wouldn't be necessary.

He stopped the car in the circular drive and looked around. It was pitch-dark now, but there were enough security and Christmas lights for him to see that no one was lurking around, ready to strike. Still, he didn't want to dawdle. Grayson grabbed the suitcase that

Eve had taken from her place in San Antonio. She latched on to the laptop, and they hurried up the flagstone porch steps.

Other than the Christmas lights, there was no glitz here like at the Collier estate. The porch was painted white, and the rocking chairs weren't just for show. They used them often.

"You're finally here," Bessie said the moment she threw open the door. And despite the laptop between them, Bessie hugged Eve. "Girl, you are a sight for sore eyes."

"It's great to see you, too, Bessie," Eve answered.

"I got a room all made up for you." Bessie caught on to Eve's arm and led her across the foyer. Not marble, but Texas hardwood.

The furnishings here and in the rest of the house leaned more toward a Western theme with pine tables and oil paintings of the various show horses and livestock they'd had over the years. One of Dade's girlfriends had joked that it was cowboy chic.

Eve glanced around and took a deep breath. She was probably thinking things hadn't changed much since she'd last been here. Grayson's thoughts went in a different direction. As always, she looked as if she belonged there.

Under different circumstances, she would have.

But it hadn't been different circumstances since his father had walked out on his family twenty years ago. Since then Grayson hadn't wanted a wife or a family. Of course, that hadn't stopped him from having sex with Eve in the woods.

Later, he'd have to figure out how to deal with that.

Bessie directed Eve toward the stairs to the right of the entry. "I can run you a bath. And then you can have something to eat. I made chili and pecan pie, your favorites."

Eve looked back at Grayson as if she expected him to rescue her. "I need to go over these pictures," she insisted.

Grayson took the laptop from her, balancing it in his left hand since he had her suitcase in his right. "The pictures can wait a few minutes. Besides, I'm starving. Take your bath so we can eat."

That wasn't exactly true. Eve and he had grabbed some fast food on the way out to the Collier estate, but Grayson knew he could get Eve's cooperation if she thought the dinner and bath breaks were for him and not her.

It worked. Eve didn't argue.

While Bessie chattered away about the Christmas dinner plans, she led Eve into the bathroom of the guest suite. Grayson deposited Eve's suitcase in the bedroom and went to his suite directly across the hall so he, too, could grab a quick shower.

Grayson tossed his clothes and Stetson onto the bed and hurried because he wanted to get back to the pictures. He also needed to find out the status of the background checks on Annabel, Claude, Sebastian and Nina. However, he wasn't nearly as quick as Eve because he had barely dried off and put on a pair of clean jeans when there was a knock at the door.

"It's me," Eve said, but she didn't wait. She threw open the door just as Grayson was zipping his jeans.

"Oh, sorry," she mumbled. Her hair was wet, no makeup, and she was wearing a dark green sweater top and pants. She wasn't wearing shoes but rather a pair of socks.

She fluttered her fingers behind her as if indicating that she was about to return to her room so he could finish dressing. But she stayed put with her gaze pinned to his bare chest and stomach.

She pulled in her breath and held it for a second. "You have a scar," she whispered.

For a moment Grayson had thought that breathless reaction was for his half-naked body. It's a good thing it wasn't.

And he was pretty sure he believed that.

She walked toward him, slowly, leaned down and touched the six-inch scar that started at his chest and ended on his right side. "How did it happen?"

"I broke up a fight at the cantina on the edge of town. Didn't see the switchblade until it was too late."

Another deep breath. "You could have been killed." Her voice was suddenly clogged with emotion.

Yeah. But Grayson kept that to himself. He also caught her hand to move it off his stomach, but somehow their fingers ended up laced together.

And neither of them pulled away.

Their eyes met. She was so familiar to him, but those eyes always held a surprise or two. Sometimes they were a misty blue. Other times, the color of a spring Texas sky.

Grayson cursed that last analogy.

He was a cowboy, and the last thing he should be doing was thinking poetic thoughts about the color of Eve's eyes.

His thoughts weren't so poetic when it came to the rest of her.

Grayson knew exactly how she looked beneath those winter clothes. He knew how much she liked it when he kissed her belly.

And the inside of her thighs. He knew the way she smelled. The way she tasted. The sounds that she made when he was driving her hot and crazy. And it was because he knew all those things that he had to back away.

But he didn't.

They stood there, gazes locked, as if paralysis had set in and neither could move. Eve's breath became thin. Her face flushed. She glanced at his bed, and Grayson knew exactly what she was thinking.

He'd made love to her in that bed.

Things had been different then. Ten years ago they'd remodeled the house and turned all the bedrooms into suites. But the black lacquered wrought-iron bed was the same. It'd been his grandfather's, and Grayson had staked claim to it twenty years ago after his grandfather had been killed. He'd gone through several mattresses in those twenty years, but the bed itself had remained unchanged.

No telling how many times Grayson had sneaked Eve up to his room. To this very bed.

In the beginning, neither had had a clue what they were doing. They had followed their instincts. Did the things that felt good. And plenty of those times, he'd had to kiss her hard and deep to muffle the sounds she made when she climaxed.

Grayson could hear those sounds now echoing through his head.

He couldn't help but respond to those memories. To the touch of her fingers linked with his.

Part of him, the part straining against the zipper of his jeans, started to rationalize that he could put her on that bed again. He knew how to get those sounds from her. Knew the delicious heat of her body.

"Mercy," she mumbled, but it didn't have any sound. She shook her head. Moistened her lips.

He wanted to hear her voice. Those sounds. But most of all, he just wanted to kiss her.

"It would be a mistake," Grayson said more to himself than her.

"Oh, yeah. A big one." But she inched closer. So close that he tasted her breath on his mouth. That taste went straight through him.

Something inside him snapped, and he latched on to the back of her neck and hauled her to him. Their mouths met, and he heard the sound all right. A little bit of whimper mixed with a boatload of relief.

Grayson knew exactly how she felt.

Helpless. Stupid.

And hot.

"Should I close the door and give you time alone?" someone snarled from the doorway. It was his brother Mason.

Eve and Grayson flew apart as if they'd just been caught doing something wrong. Which was true. They couldn't lust after each other. Sex against the tree to make a baby was one thing. But real sex would turn their status from *it's complicated* to *it's damn impossible.*

"Well?" Mason prompted in that surly non-interested way that only Mason could manage. "You need time to do something about that kiss or what?"

"Did you want something?" Grayson fired back at his brother.

Mason lifted the papers he had in his hand and dropped them onto the table near the door. "Background reports on the Colliers and the dead girl. You should read them. There's some interesting stuff in there." He tipped his head to the laptop. "Anything with the photos?"

"Not yet," Eve and Grayson said in unison.

If that frustrated Mason, he didn't show it. He turned but then stopped. "Good to see you, Eve." From Mason, that was a warm, fuzzy welcome.

"It's good to see you, too." Eve's was considerably warmer. Strange, most people steered clear of Mason, but Eve went to him and planted a kiss on his cheek.

Now Mason looked uncomfortable. "Yell if you need me." And with that mumbled offer, he strolled away.

Both Eve and he hurried to the reports that Mason had dropped on the table, and Grayson snatched them up. There were at least thirty pages, and with Eve right at his shoulder, they started to skim through them. It didn't take long for Grayson to see what Mason had considered *interesting stuff.*

There was a photo of Claude's first wife, Cicely, and it was the same woman in the photos taken in his office. So that was one thing cleared up. Claude's ex had visited him. Nothing suspicious about that. Since she was the mother of his son, they would always have a connection.

That required Grayson to take a deep breath because he couldn't help but think that one day, soon, Eve and he might have that same connection.

"Cicely had twins," Eve read, touching her finger to that part of the background. "Sebastian and Sophia."

This was the first Grayson had heard of it, but then he'd only had a preliminary report of Sebastian before the interview at the Collier estate.

Grayson read on. "When Sophia was six months old, the nanny, Helen Bolton, disappeared with her, and even though Helen turned up dead three months later, Sophia was never found."

On the same page of the report, there was a photo of baby Sophia that had obviously been taken right before she went missing.

"You have a scanner in the house?" Eve asked, her attention nailed to the picture of the baby.

"Sure. In my office."

Eve grabbed the laptop and headed up the hall. She practically raced ahead of him, and the moment they were inside, she fed the picture into the scanner and loaded it onto the laptop with the other photos they'd gotten from Annabel.

"What are you doing?" Grayson wanted to know.

While she typed frantically on the keyboard, Eve sank down in the leather chair behind his desk. "I have age progression software. It's not a hundred percent accurate, but it might work."

Grayson watched Eve manipulate the copied image of the baby, and soon it began to take shape. The adult version of Sophia Collier appeared on the screen.

Grayson cursed under his breath. The hair was different, but there were enough similarities.

"Oh, God," Eve mumbled. She leaned away from the laptop and touched her fingers to her mouth. "Do you see it?" she asked.

"Yeah." Grayson saw it all right.

And it meant this investigation had just taken a crazy twist.

Because the dead woman, Nina Manning, hadn't been Claude's mistress as they'd originally thought. She was Sophia Collier, Claude's missing daughter.

Chapter 12

"I wished you'd stayed at the ranch," Grayson mumbled again. He kept his attention pinned to the San Antonio downtown street that was clogged with holiday shoppers and traffic.

Eve ignored him. She'd already explained her reasons for tagging along for this visit to Cicely Collier. She wanted the truth about the dead woman, and when that happened, the danger would be over. She could go home and, well, wait until she could take a pregnancy test.

It had been less than twenty-four hours since Grayson had agreed to have sex with her, but she'd read enough of the pregnancy books to know that conception could have already happened.

She could be pregnant.

Despite everything else going on, Eve smiled and slid her hand over her stomach. Even though it was a long shot, she wanted to hang on to the possibility as long as she could.

Even if she couldn't hang on to Grayson.

That kiss in his bedroom had felt so much like old times, and as stupid as it sounded, it had felt more intimate than the sex. It had been real, not some gesture that she'd had to talk Grayson into doing.

And that's why it couldn't happen again.

She could coax him into kissing her again. Maybe even talk him into coming to her bed. But he would soon feel trapped, and he would blame himself—and her—for feeling that way. She cared for him too much to make him go through that. Grayson already had enough duty forced on him in his life without making him feel even a shred of obligation to her. More kissing would make him feel obligated.

"You okay?" Grayson asked.

She glanced at him and realized he'd seen her hand on her stomach. "I'm fine."

He seemed suspicious of her answer, but he didn't press it. Nor would he. A discussion about the baby was off-limits for both of them, and Eve was thankful for it. Conversation wasn't going to help with this matter. No. The only thing that would help was to put some distance between them.

The voice on the GPS directed them toward another turn, and Grayson drove into the upscale San Antonio neighborhood. Of course, she hadn't expected Cicely to live in a shack, but it was obvious the woman had done well in the divorce settlement.

Grayson parked in the driveway of the two-story Victorian-style home. It was painted a soft buttery yellow with white trim, and despite the fact that it was the dead of winter, the lawn was as pristine as the house.

"I have a warrant for Cicely's DNA," Grayson explained, grabbing the large padded envelope that earlier he'd put on the backseat. "I can compare it to Nina's. If it's a match, we'll have proof that Nina is really Sophia Collier."

"What about Claude's DNA?" Eve asked.

"There's a warrant for that, too. Nate's over there now collecting it."

Poor Nate. She doubted Claude would make the process easy. For that matter, maybe Cicely wouldn't either, especially when they told her that her long-lost daughter was likely dead. Murdered, at that.

Eve was bracing herself for the worst.

Grayson and she got out of the car and went to the door. Unlike at the Collier estate, Cicely already had the door open and was waiting for them.

Cicely looked exactly as she had in the photographs that Annabel had taken of her in Claude's office. Her short, dark brown hair was perfect, not a strand out of place, and she wore a simple olive-green wool suit. She was nothing like Annabel, her curvy young replacement, but it was easy to see that Cicely had once been stunningly beautiful.

"Sheriff Ryland," Cicely greeted. Her nerves were there in her voice and the worry etched on her face.

"Mrs. Collier. This is Eve Warren. She's helping with the investigation."

"Yes." She stared at Eve and repeated it. "Sebastian called and told me that Ms. Warren had taken a picture that you have some questions about."

Cicely stepped back, motioning for them to enter. She didn't say anything else until she led into a cozy room off the back of the foyer. The painting over the stone fireplace immediately caught Eve's eye. It was an oil painting of two babies. One was definitely Sophia, and she guessed the other one was Sebastian.

"My children," Cicely explained, following Eve's gaze. "Won't you please have a seat?" She motioned toward the pair of chairs.

There was a gleaming silver tray with a teapot and cookies on the coffee table. Cicely sat on a floral sofa and began to serve them. Eve sat across from her.

"Sebastian dropped by earlier, and we had a long chat." Cicely's hands were trembling when she passed Eve the tea that she'd poured in a delicate cup painted with yellow roses. "He's worried. And so am I. You think Sebastian had something to do with Nina Manning's death."

"Did he?" Grayson asked. He waved off the tea when Cicely offered it to him and sat in the chair next to Eve.

"No." Cicely's pale green eyes came to Eve's. "But of course, that means nothing. I would say that because he's my son."

Eve was more than a little surprised that a mother would admit that. Of course, despite her comment about *being worried,* maybe Cicely and Sebastian weren't that close.

Grayson took out the warrant and the DNA kit from the envelope and handed them to Cicely. "I need a sample of your DNA."

Cicely's forehead bunched up, and for a moment Eve thought she would refuse, but she only refused the warrant. She pushed it aside, took the swab and without questions, she used it on the inside of her mouth.

"It's not necessary, you know," she said, handing the kit back to Grayson.

Yes, it was, and Eve figured Grayson was about to tell her why. Eve held her breath.

"Mrs. Collier—" But that was as far as Grayson got.

"Yes," Cicely interrupted. "I know that Nina Manning is…was my daughter."

Eve didn't know who looked more surprised—Grayson or her.

Cicely took a sip of tea, but her hand was trembling so much that some of it sloshed into the saucer. "I've already done the DNA test, and I can provide a copy of the results if you need them."

Grayson stayed quiet a moment. "How long have you known that she was your daughter?"

Cicely dodged his gaze. "About a month."

"A month?" Grayson mumbled something under his breath. "And you didn't think you should tell the police that your kidnapped daughter had returned?"

"I considered many things but not that." Cicely let the vague comment hang in the air for several seconds. "About a month ago, Nina showed up here and claimed to be Sophia. She said that as a baby she'd been abandoned at a church and had been raised in foster care. I didn't believe her, of course. Not until I got back the results from the DNA test."

Cicely blinked back tears. "I thought my daughter was dead."

After twenty-two years, that was reasonable, but Eve knew if she'd been in Cicely's shoes, she would have never stopped looking. *Never.*

"What happened when you found out Nina was telling the truth?" Grayson asked.

Balancing her cup on her lap, she picked at a nonexistent piece of lint on her jacket. "I begged her to come home. It was obvious that she needed help. Rehab. Counseling. Did you know that she'd been selling her body to support her drug habit?"

Grayson nodded. "She had a record."

Cicely pulled in her breath as if it were physically painful to hear her suspicions confirmed. "She refused my help. She only wanted money, and I didn't want to hand over cash because I knew she'd just use it for drugs. So I called Claude to see if he would help me convince her to go to rehab."

Grayson and Eve exchanged a glance.

"Claude knew that Nina was your daughter?" Grayson asked.

"Of course," Cicely said without hesitation. "What? Did he deny it?"

"He did," Grayson confirmed.

Her mouth tightened. "Well, apparently he wasn't just a weasel of a husband, he's also a weasel of a father." She practically dumped her teacup onto the table and got up. She folded her arms over her chest and paced. "Did you meet his new tart of a wife?"

"Yes, we met Annabel." Grayson didn't say a word about the photos Annabel had provided. Without them, it might have taken a lot longer to make the connection between Nina and Sophia. However, Eve wasn't sure that had been Annabel's intention.

"Annabel." Cicely repeated the name like it was a profanity. "You can put her at the top of the list of suspects as my daughter's killer. She probably hired her lapdog, Leon Ames, to murder my baby in cold blood."

Eve set her tea aside also. This conversation was definitely loaded with bombshells. "Why would Annabel do that?" Eve wanted to know.

Cicely rubbed her fingers together. "Money, plain and simple. Claude's dying, you know?"

Grayson shook his head. "You're sure?"

"Positive. Sebastian told me all about it. Claude has a malignant nonoperable brain tumor. Probably has less than two months to live. And when they put Claude in the ground, the tart will inherit half of his estate. If Sophia had lived, the split would have been three ways. Apparently, that wasn't enough money for her."

Mercy. If that was true, then Cicely had not only just given Annabel a motive but Sebastian, as well. After all, Sebastian certainly hadn't volunteered anything about the dead woman being his sister. In fact, he'd lied to Grayson from the very start.

"I need to re-interview Claude and Sebastian," Grayson said, standing.

"Annabel, too," Cicely insisted. "She's the one who had my baby killed, and I'm going to prove it. I want her surgically perfected butt tossed in jail."

Cicely wasn't so shaky now. She looked like a woman on a mission of revenge.

"You need to stay out of the investigation," Grayson reminded her. "If Annabel is guilty, I'll figure out a way to prove it."

Cicely didn't respond, and Eve wondered just how much trouble the woman would be. She wasn't just going to drop this.

"You can see yourselves out," Cicely said with ice in her voice. She'd apparently worked herself into a frenzy and was no longer in the hostess mode.

Grayson and Eve did just that. They saw themselves out, but Eve was reeling from what they'd just learned. Reeling and frustrated.

"I thought by now we'd have just one suspect," Eve whispered to Grayson on the way to the door. "Instead we have two—Annabel and Sebastian."

"We have four," Grayson whispered back, and he didn't say more until they were outside. "Claude might not have been so happy to see his drug-addicted, prostitute daughter return to the family fold."

True. He had a thing about keeping mud off his good name. "And the fourth suspect?"

Grayson opened the car door for her, and she got inside. "Cicely."

Eve shook her head. "You think she would kill her own daughter?"

"I don't know, but I'm going to find out." He shut her door, got in behind the wheel and drove away. He took a deep breath. "I could drop you off at SAPD headquarters while I re-interview the Colliers."

Eve gave him a flat look. "I'm going with you."

Grayson matched her look and added a

raised eyebrow. "There could be a killer in the house."

She wasn't immune to the fear, mainly because Eve believed that one of the Colliers was indeed a killer. But she was stuck on this investigation treadmill until Grayson made an arrest. Eve wanted to confront the danger head-on, and the sooner that happened, the better.

Grayson mumbled something about her being stubborn and grabbed his phone. "Then I'll have Nate bring the Colliers into the police station."

Eve didn't have to guess how this would play out. "They aren't going to like that."

"Good. Because I don't like the lies they've told us. Plus, I'd like to see how Claude reacts when I show him the memory card his wife gave us."

Eve almost felt sorry for Annabel. *Almost.* But then, Annabel did have a strong motive for murder—her soon-to-be-dead husband's money. And it was as if Annabel was trying to put the blame on either Claude or her stepson with those pictures she'd taken.

Grayson made the call to Nate, and while he was arranging the follow-up interview with the Colliers, Eve grabbed her laptop because she wanted to continue studying the photos. Before she could do that, however, she noticed the email from her doctor, Alan Stephenson.

The message was simple. "I've been trying to reach you. Call me."

Eve automatically reached for her cell, only to remember she didn't have one. It was in Grayson's truck, which had gone into the creek. She hadn't checked her answering machine at the condo either, mainly because Grayson had been in such a hurry to get her out of there.

"I need to use your phone," she told Grayson the moment he ended his call with Nate.

"Anything wrong?" he asked.

"I'm not sure." Eve took the cell and frantically pressed in the phone number at the bottom of the email. A dozen things went through her mind, most of them bad. Had the doctor been wrong about her ovulating? Had she put Grayson through all of this for nothing? Her heart broke at the thought of her being too late to have a child of her own.

She got the doctor's answering service first, but Dr. Stephenson had left word to put her call through to him. Moments later, the doctor picked up.

"Eve," he greeted, but she could hear something in his voice. This was not good news.

"I got your email. You've been trying to call me?"

"Most of yesterday afternoon. I found a private sperm donor, but as you probably already know, it's already too late. I'm sorry."

Her lungs were aching so she released the breath she'd been holding. "I found a donor." She didn't look at Grayson, but she sensed he was looking at her.

"That's wonderful." The doctor sounded both surprised and relieved. "Did you use artificial insemination?"

The image of Grayson in the woods flashed through her mind. "No. There wasn't time."

The doctor cleared his throat. "Well, the old-fashioned way works, too."

And was a lot more pleasurable. But Eve kept that to herself. "I know it's probably a long shot."

"Maybe not. Having sex when you're ovulating substantially increases the odds. Come in next week, and I'll run a test. We should be able to tell if you're pregnant."

Everything inside Eve began to spin. "Next week? That soon?"

"That soon," the doctor assured her. "Call the office and make an appointment. I'll see you then."

The doctor ended the call, and Eve just sat

there and stared at the phone. It was exactly the news she wanted. The doctor was hopeful that she had conceived, and she wouldn't have to wait long. Seven days. That was it. And she would know if Grayson and she had made a baby.

But she immediately shook her head. She couldn't think of this as Grayson's baby.

Only hers.

"My doctor can do the pregnancy test next week," she relayed to Grayson, though he was looking at everything but her now.

He didn't respond. Which was just as well. Best not to mention pregnancy tests or the baby again because if this interview with the Colliers went well, maybe Grayson could make an arrest. Then, they would go their separate ways.

That stung.

But it was necessary. A baby had to be enough. She couldn't go weaving a fantasy life with Grayson when the last thing he wanted was to raise another child.

Eve cursed the tears that sprang to her eyes, and then she cursed Grayson for being able to detach so easily. She glanced at him to see if he'd had any reaction whatsoever to the test news, but he was volleying his attention between the street ahead and the rearview mirror.

That wasn't a detached look on his face.

"What's wrong?" she asked, turning in her seat to follow his gaze.

He reached inside his jacket and drew his gun. "Someone's following us."

Chapter 13

Next week

The timing of Eve's pregnancy results should have been the last thing on Grayson's mind, but he was having a hard time pushing it aside.

"That dark blue car is the one following us?" Eve asked. She apparently wasn't thinking baby tests, either. She had her attention on the vehicle behind them.

"Yeah." It wasn't right on their tail, but the blue car had stayed several vehicles back and had made the last three turns that Grayson had taken.

"Can you see the driver?" she asked.

"No." The noon sun was catching the tint

of the windows at the wrong angle, and Grayson couldn't even tell how many people there were in the car. Heck, he wasn't positive they were even being followed.

So Grayson did a test of his own.

Without signaling, he took a right turn so quickly that the driver behind him honked. But Grayson got his answer. The blue car made the same turn.

"What now?" There was a tremble in Eve's voice, and it had been that way since she'd spoken to her doctor. But now it was heavy with concern.

"We drive to SAPD headquarters as planned." Grayson only hoped the car followed them into the parking lot so he could confront this moron. Of course, he didn't want to do that with Eve around, but maybe he could get her inside the headquarters building first.

Grayson made his way through the side streets and spotted the SAPD parking lot just ahead. He pulled in, heading straight toward the drop-off that would put Eve just a few yards from the front door.

"The driver didn't turn," Eve relayed.

A glance in the rearview mirror verified that. Maybe this idiot hadn't wanted to risk arrest, but that didn't mean he wouldn't follow them when they left. Grayson would have to take extra precautions. He damn sure didn't want someone trying to shoot out their tires again.

"I'll park and be inside in a minute," Grayson told Eve and was thankful she didn't argue with him about that. The instant he came to a stop, Eve hurried inside the building.

Nate was there, just inside the door waiting for her, and Grayson caught a glimpse of Nate pulling her into his arms for a hug. It was ironic. His brothers had always loved Eve, had always thought of her as part of the family. How would they react if it turned out that she was indeed pregnant with his child?

Grayson groaned.

Maybe the better question was, how would *he* react?

Well, next week he'd know. By then, he'd hopefully have Nina Manning's killer behind bars and would be able to have some time to think this all through.

He parked and went inside to join Eve and Nate who were waiting for him in the reception area.

"Eve said someone was following you?" Nate asked.

"Yeah. But he apparently got cold feet. I got a description but not the plates."

Nate's forehead bunched up. "When you

get ready to take Eve back to the ranch, I'll have one of the cruisers accompany you. That should deter anyone from following or launching another attack."

You'd think, but this investigation was twisting and turning too much for Grayson's liking. He just wanted it to end so that Eve could be safe.

"Sebastian Collier is already here," Nate announced, leading them through the headquarters toward the interview rooms. "Claude and Annabel are on the way."

"Did they give you any hassle about coming?" Eve asked.

The flat look Nate gave her indicated they had. "Claude says he'll sue us for harassment."

Grayson figured the man would use that threat, but if the DNA proved that Nina was his biological child, then that might get SAPD authorization for a search warrant to start going through not just the Collier estate, but Claude and Sebastian's financials. After all, someone had paid off Leon Ames, and Grayson was betting it was a Collier. Unfortunately, if they used cash, then the financial records might be a dead end.

"Eve and I can watch through the two-way mirror in the adjacent room," Nate suggested.

Both Grayson and he looked at Eve, and she opened her mouth, probably to argue.

"Give yourself a break from the stress," Grayson told her, and he dropped his gaze to her stomach.

Her eyes widened and just like that, she nodded. Yeah, it was a dirty trick considering she might not even be pregnant, but there was no reason for her to go a second round with this pack of jackals. Just being in the same room with them spiked his blood pressure.

Nate maneuvered them through the maze of halls until they reached the interview room, and he took Eve next door. Sebastian was seated, but he didn't offer the smile and warm welcome that he had earlier.

"I'm assuming this is important?" Sebastian asked. Everything about his body language revealed his impatience and annoyance. His face was tight, and his breath was coming out in short bursts.

"It's important," Grayson assured him. He didn't sit. He wanted to stand so he could violate Sebastian's personal space and make him even more uncomfortable. "Did you have someone follow me a few minutes ago?"

"Please." Sebastian stretched out the syllables. "I have better things to do, like last-minute shopping. Tomorrow's Christmas Eve." He stared at them, and then he mumbled a profanity under his breath. "Look, I don't know why I'm suddenly a suspect, but I did nothing wrong."

"You lied to me."

The staring match continued, and Sebastian was the first to look away. More profanity came. "About two weeks ago Nina Manning called me and asked to meet her. She claimed she was my long-lost sister. The timing was suspicious because her call came less than twenty-four hours after my father found out he was dying."

Grayson reserved judgment on the suspicious part. "Did you meet with her?"

"Yes. At a hotel in downtown San Antonio. I didn't believe her. I thought she was running a scam, but because I didn't want her upsetting my father, I was prepared to pay her off. Then, my father showed up, and after they argued, Nina ran out."

Well, that explained Annabel's pictures. "How did your father know about the meeting?"

"Nina called him, too. I guess she figured if she couldn't get the money from me, then she'd get it from my father."

Something about this didn't sound right. "If

Nina wanted money, why did she run off after the so-called argument?"

"Because she was a drug-addicted, lying little witch," someone said from the doorway. It was Claude, and Annabel was by his side. Both looked about as thrilled to be there as Sebastian was.

Sebastian got to his feet. "You should sit, Father."

"I don't intend to be here that long," Claude fired back. "My attorney is on the way, and I've already put a call in to the mayor. I will not be treated like a common criminal." He aimed that remark and an accompanying glare at Grayson.

"Besides, Claude isn't well enough for this," Annabel added. The words were right, but the emotion didn't quite make it to her eyes. No glare for her, but she did look uncomfortable.

"A woman is dead," Grayson stated, looking at Claude. "She was last seen alive with your son and former employee. That employee tried to kill me and the woman who photographed Nina Manning." He paused. "Or maybe I should call the dead woman Sophia Collier."

"Never!" Claude's voice boomed through the hall, and with his index finger pointed at Grayson, he stepped into the room. "That piece of trash has no blood of mine in her."

Grayson shrugged. "Your ex-wife thought differently. She believed Nina was Sophia."

Annabel huffed. Now, there was real emotion. "Of course Cicely would believe that. She's mentally unstable, you know."

"She is," Sebastian agreed.

Grayson glanced at Claude to see if he had a comment about his ex, but Claude's jaw was so tight that Grayson figured he wasn't capable of speaking. Grayson made a mental note to do some digging to see if Cicely was indeed suffering from any form of mental illness.

"Since Nina's paternity is in question, we needed the DNA sample from you," Grayson told Claude.

"Which I gave," Claude spat out. "But there's no test that will convince me that she was my Sophia."

"Your son must have thought it was at least possible," Grayson disputed, "because he met with her again at the charity rodeo."

"I didn't meet with her," Sebastian insisted. "I already told you she was there with Leon. I simply ran into them."

Grayson just looked at them, waiting for an explanation he could actually believe— because he didn't buy the running into them story. His stony look didn't stop with just Sebastian, either. When Grayson let his intense stare stay on Annabel, her breath began to tremble, and she actually dropped back a step, probably because she thought she was about to be outed about the memory disk she'd given him. And Grayson considered it, but if either Sebastian or Claude was the killer, then that might make Annabel the next victim.

There was a soft knock, and since the door was still open, Grayson didn't have any trouble seeing who'd made the sound.

Cicely.

She was holding her leather purse in front of her like a shield, and she looked at them as if trying to figure out what was going on. Grayson knew how she felt.

"By any chance were you the one who followed Ms. Warren and me?" Grayson asked.

"Yes." And Cicely didn't hesitate, either. "I wanted to see if you'd run to Claude and tell him everything I said to you." She gave a smug nod. "But instead you ordered him to come here. Did he deny it?" Cicely asked, sliding her venomous gaze at Claude.

Claude had some venom of his own. The veins on his forehead and neck started to bulge. "If you're talking about that woman claiming to be Sophia, of course I denied it. She wasn't our daughter."

"I told you that I did a DNA test," Cicely said between clenched teeth.

"A test that could have been faked," Sebastian interrupted. "You're so eager to find your long-lost daughter that you're willing to believe anything."

"I faked nothing, and neither did Sophia." Cicely was so angry now that she was shaking, and she opened her purse and snatched something from it. Something encased in a plastic zip bag. She slapped it onto the table.

Grayson walked closer to see what it was. He'd expected a photo or something else that might shed light on this.

But it was a diamond bracelet.

Grayson frowned. "Is this connected to the investigation?"

"It is." Cicely pointed to Annabel. "She gave the bracelet to Sophia as a bribe to get her to leave."

Annabel, Sebastian and Claude all disagreed, and they weren't quiet about it, either. "I've never seen that bracelet before," Annabel insisted. She reached for the bag, but Cicely snagged her wrist.

"Sophia said you gave it to her and demanded that she sell it and use the money to get out of town. I sealed it up because I'm betting the police can find your DNA on it."

Maybe. But that wouldn't prove anything other than perhaps Annabel had told him another lie. It didn't mean she was a killer.

"How did you get the bracelet?" Grayson asked Cicely.

And with that one simple question, the room fell silent, and all eyes were on Cicely.

Cicely lifted her chin as if insulted by the implication of the question. "When Sophia came to my house, she had the bracelet with her and said it was a bribe from Annabel. She also said she was scared, that she thought Annabel would kill her if she didn't leave town and not try to stake a claim to her rightful inheritance."

"It's only a rightful claim if she was my sister," Sebastian tossed at her. "And she wasn't."

That started up another round of accusations, and Cicely was loud and liberal with the name calling—especially the names she called Annabel.

"Shut up!" Grayson practically yelled. And he turned back to Cicely. "Why would Sophia leave the bracelet with you?"

Cicely didn't jump to answer that. In fact, she swallowed hard. "She didn't say, exactly, but I think she knew something bad was going to happen to her. I think she wanted me to have it so I could prove that Annabel was her killer."

Annabel gasped and caught on to Grayson's arm. "I didn't kill her. I..." But she didn't finish, and the grip she had on his arm melted away. "I didn't kill her," she repeated.

Sebastian moved closer as if checking to make sure Annabel was okay. When his attention came back to Cicely, his eyes were narrowed. "Mother, why don't you tell the sheriff about your association with Leon Ames?"

"Association?" Cicely pulled back her shoulders. "I don't know what you mean."

"Really?" Sebastian challenged. He walked toward his mother. Slow, calculated steps. "Leon visited you often. In fact, he visited you in the past week."

Cicely didn't deny it, and when she tried to look away, Grayson got right in her face. "Is it true?"

The woman finally nodded, prompting an I-told-you-so huff from Sebastian. Neither Annabel nor Claude seemed surprised with Cicely's admission, which meant they had likely known.

"Leon was my friend." Cicely's voice was practically a whisper.

Friend. That was an interesting relationship, especially considering Leon worked for

Claude. Of course, that didn't mean he hadn't been secretly working for Cicely, as well. Since Grayson believed that Leon had likely killed Nina, now he had to figure out who had given the man orders to kill.

"Leon was your lover and would have done anything for you," Sebastian accused. He was smirking when he looked at Grayson. "My mother has an affinity for associating with lowlifes. That's probably why she was so eager to believe that woman when she claimed she was Sophia."

That put some fire back into Cicely, and she opened her mouth, probably to verbally blast her son into the next county.

But a sound stopped her.

A gasp.

Not just any ordinary gasp, either. It was as if all the air swooshed out of Claude's lungs.

"Sebastian," Claude managed to say. A split second before he clamped his hands to the sides of his head and dropped to the floor.

Chapter 14

Eve got out of Grayson's car and made her way up the steps of the ranch house. Despite the fact that someone had tried to kill them twice today, her nerves were no longer firing on all cylinders.

Thank God.

The bone-weary fatigue was no doubt responsible for that. The Christmas lights helped, too. Hard to think of murders and attacks when there were hundreds of multi-colored lights twinkling around her. And then she stepped inside and knew this was the main source of her calmer nerves.

For reasons she didn't want to explore, the Ryland ranch always had and always would feel like home to her. So many memories, and they flooded through her, easing away the rest of the tension.

Grayson walked in right behind her. He had his phone sandwiched between his ear and shoulder, a place it'd been during most of their drive from San Antonio back to the ranch. Along the way, he'd gotten several updates on the investigation.

And Claude.

Judging from the part of this particular conversation, Grayson was talking with Claude's doctor.

When the man had first collapsed at the SAPD precinct, Eve had thought he was faking it so he could put a quick end to the interview. But after he'd been rushed to the hospital in an ambulance, the doctors had informed Grayson that Claude's condition was critical. So, no more interviews until the man was stable. Whenever that would be.

"Claude is still touch and go," Grayson relayed to her when he ended the call. "He might not make it through the night." He slapped his phone shut and pulled in a long, weary breath.

Eve understood that weariness. She wasn't fond of Claude, but if he died, he might take his secrets to the grave. Especially one secret.

Had he been the one responsible for Nina's death?

Or did that guilt lie with Sebastian, Annabel or even Cicely?

"What about the DNA results?" Eve wanted to know because she'd heard Grayson's phone conversation with Nate about that, as well.

Grayson shook his head. "Nothing yet, but we should have preliminary results in an hour or two." He used the keypad on the wall to arm the security system. "Nate's also checking to see if anyone else, including Cicely, ran a DNA test on Nina."

She thought about that for a moment. "But Cicely said she'd done the test. Why would she lie about something like that?"

"Who knows? I'm still working that out, but I'm not ready to believe anything a Collier says."

Eve agreed. All of them seemed to have something to hide, but the DNA results might be a start toward learning the truth. If Nina was indeed Sophia, then that only strengthened Sebastian and Annabel's motives for murder. They might not have wanted to split Claude's estate three ways.

Still, there were some things Eve hadn't been able to grasp. "I understand why Claude might have had Nina killed," she commented.

"With his elitist attitude, he would never admit to having a drug addict daughter. But what about Cicely? She seems more than willing to admit that Nina was hers. So, why would she kill her?"

"Seems," Grayson emphasized. "That's why I want to see when and if Cicely ran the DNA test."

Ah, Eve got it then. Because the test could have been a cover-up. Nina could have confronted or even attempted to blackmail Cicely, and Cicely could have refused to believe this was her long-lost daughter. Cicely could have had Nina killed out of anger. However, the woman wouldn't look like a major murder suspect if she told everyone that she knew Nina was truly Sophia.

If Cicely had done that, it was a smart move.

"Anyone home?" Grayson called out. When no one answered, he headed for the kitchen, and Eve followed.

She immediately spotted the note from Bessie on the double-door stainless-steel fridge. "Mason called. He and Dade are staying in town to work on the case," Grayson read aloud. "Nate and the baby won't be home, either. Haven't heard a peep from Kade. Dinner's in the fridge and I'm headed out for girls' night at my sister's place in Saddle Springs.

Grayson

Give Eve a good-night kiss for me." Bessie had added a smiley face.

The woman's attempt at humor didn't cause either Grayson or Eve to smile. But it did give Eve an uneasy feeling because she realized that Grayson and she were alone in the house. She glanced at Grayson, and his quick look away convinced her that he was aware of it, as well.

"You'll need to eat," he reminded her.

"You, too," she reminded him right back.

But neither of them moved. They both stood there, staring at Bessie's note, while the air zinged around them. For a moment Eve wondered if Grayson might act on that good-night kiss after all, but he mumbled something about being hungry and pulled open the fridge door.

There was a large baking dish with lasagna on the center shelf. She was suddenly starving. She knew from experience that Bessie was an amazing cook, but Eve decided both Grayson and she could use a little space to clear their heads. After all, in the past twenty-four hours, they'd nearly been killed and had then gotten embroiled in a murder investigation.

They'd also had sex.

Even the fatigue couldn't erase the too-familiar tingling she still felt. And that was another huge reason for a little head-clearing space.

"I think I'll take a shower before I eat," Eve told him.

Grayson didn't have time to respond because his cell phone rang. Eve waited just a few seconds to make sure it wasn't critical, but when she realized it was the youngest Ryland, Kade, calling for an update about the investigation, she excused herself and went to the guest suite.

Eve intended to head straight for the shower, but she saw the photo album on the guest bed. The leather cover had probably once been white but had aged to a rich cream color, and it was thick, at least three inches.

"Here's your Christmas present. Thought you'd like copies of some old memories," was written on the sticky note attached. "Love, Bessie."

She was reasonably sure she didn't need any more memories or copies of memories, but Eve sat on the edge of the bed and opened it. The first picture was of Boone and Marcie Ryland, Grayson's parents, on their wedding day. They were both smiling, and there were no hints of the troubles to come nineteen years later when Boone would walk out on Marcie and his six sons. A few months after that, Marcie would take her own life.

What a waste. So many lives had been changed because of Boone's departure. Especially Grayson's. If he hadn't had to raise his brothers, he might have wanted a family of his own. But it hurt Eve too much to dwell on that particular *if*.

Eve turned the page to Grayson's baby picture—probably taken when he was no more than a day or two old. She smiled. If she was indeed pregnant, then this was a glimpse of how her baby could look.

She flipped through the pages, each of them snapshots of time. Grayson's first horseback ride—barely a toddler in the saddle. His first day of school.

And then Eve was in the picture—literally.

Nearly all the subsequent pages had photos of her with the Ryland family. Christmas. Easter. Birthdays. She'd been a part of them. Always engulfed in those strong arms that had always given her so much love.

She ached to be part of that again but knew it was lost forever. The ultimatum she'd given Grayson all those years ago had sealed her fate and separated her from him, and his family, forever.

Or had it?

Her mind began to spin with the possibility of her baby being part of this. Not permanently part of the family but maybe visits so the baby would know his or her bloodline.

But she forced herself to stop.

She'd made the deal with Grayson—if he got her pregnant, that would be it. No strings attached. So, her fate was sealed. Her baby's fate, too. One way or another, she would leave as soon as it was safe.

Eve blinked back tears, but more followed. She was still swiping them away when the house phone rang. She glanced at the caller ID screen and saw that it was Annabel Collier. Since this could be important, she lay the album aside and hurried downstairs.

Grayson was in the kitchen where he was already talking to Annabel, and he had put the call on speaker. "I'm listening," he said to Annabel.

Annabel didn't say anything for several seconds. "I'm not sure how to say this."

Grayson huffed. "Try," he insisted. He looked at Eve then, and his right eyebrow slid up, questioning her about something. When she shook her head, Grayson went to her and touched her cheek. Or so she thought. But not a real touch. He wiped away a stray tear.

"You okay?" he mouthed.

Eve moved away from him, and thankfully didn't have to explain anything because Annabel continued.

"I lied to you," the woman confessed.

Grayson didn't huff this time, but he looked as if he wanted to do just that. "Which lie would that be?"

"About the diamond bracelet. It was mine. I figured you would discover that when you had it tested so I decided to come clean. I gave it to Nina, hoping it would convince her to leave."

Now Eve was the one to huff. The Colliers were certainly free with their lies, and she didn't think it was a coincidence that the lies seemed to be attempts to prevent them from being charged with murder.

"Then Cicely was right." Grayson took out a plate of heated lasagna from the microwave and handed it to Eve.

"Cicely was trying to make me sound guilty. That's the only reason she had the bracelet. She wants to incriminate me."

Eve got them both out some silverware and paper napkins and sat at the counter. Grayson got out two longneck beers and his plate. He looked at her. Studied her. Maybe trying to figure out what had caused those tears.

"The question you should be asking yourself is how Cicely got that bracelet in the first place," Annabel went on. "Because I seriously doubt Nina freely gave it to her. That bracelet was worth thousands, and a druggie like Nina wouldn't have handed it over without a fight."

"Are you saying Cicely killed Nina and took the bracelet?" Grayson didn't wait. He sat and started to eat.

"Yes, that's exactly what I'm saying." But then Annabel paused. "Or maybe Sebastian killed her and gave the bracelet to his mother. He could have done it to try to incriminate me, too."

"Sebastian," Grayson repeated. "I wondered when this conversation would turn to him."

"What do you mean?" Annabel accused.

He had a gulp of beer first. And another look at Eve. "I mean your husband is dying. By tomorrow morning, you could be a wealthy widow—thanks to your huge inheritance. If Sebastian were out of the picture, you'd have double the wealth and no pesky stepchildren around to cash in on their daddy's will."

Annabel made a sound of outrage. "I didn't kill anyone!" she practically shouted.

"Maybe. Can you say the same for your husband?" Grayson challenged.

Silence. The moments crawled by, and Grayson continued to sip his beer. The glances at her continued, too. What didn't happen was a denial from Annabel about her husband's innocence.

"If Claude recovers, you'll have to ask him that." Annabel's voice was no longer hot with anger. It was ice-cold and impatient.

"I will," Grayson assured her. "Now, tell me why you gave me the memory card with the photos."

She paused again. "Because I knew something wasn't right when Nina showed up. Claude and Sebastian were having secret conversations. And Cicely kept calling. I didn't know Nina was going to die, but I thought I might need proof."

"Proof of what?" Grayson pressed.

"That I didn't have anything to do with her, her life or her death."

"Well, the pictures don't prove that." Of course, they did prove that all their suspects had had close contact with a woman who was murdered. Even if Annabel hadn't taken the pictures herself, she had certainly been aware of them.

"I didn't kill her," Annabel insisted. "Now that I've told you about the bracelet, we have nothing further to discuss." And she hung up.

Without taking his attention off Eve, he leaned over and pressed the end button on the phone. Since his stare was making her uncomfortable, Eve focused on the square of lasagna in front of her.

"Why are you looking at me like that?" she finally asked.

Grayson opened his mouth. Closed it. And the staring continued.

Eve decided she'd just spill it. "I was crying because I'd been looking at a photo album that Bessie gave me for Christmas. Old memories," she settled for saying.

"Oh." And judging from his tone, that was not the answer he'd expected. "I thought maybe...well, I thought you'd learned you weren't pregnant."

Now, it was her turn to say "Oh." He'd seen the tears and assumed the worst. Or maybe in his case, the best—that maybe she'd gotten her period. However, that wouldn't be just bad news. It would break her heart.

"No." Since the lasagna suddenly wasn't settling well in her stomach, Eve got up so she could put it back in the fridge. "I won't know until next week."

"Okay." He nodded, repeated it.

She could feel his regret. His doubts. And Eve was just too tired to go there. She whirled back around to remind him that from here on out he wasn't part of her life.

But Grayson stood and whirled around at

the same time, and they practically smacked right into each other. Eve started to move back, way back, but Grayson caught on to her arm, anchoring her in place. She could have shaken off his grip, of course, but she didn't.

"I can't do this," she managed to say.

His eyebrow came up again, and he was obviously waiting for an explanation of what specifically she couldn't do, but Eve hesitated one second too long, and in that second she got caught up in Grayson's eyes. His scent.

His touch.

She'd never been able to resist him, never, and apparently tonight was no different.

"I can't, either," he answered. Though she had no idea what he meant by that.

She soon learned though.

Grayson leaned in and put his mouth on hers. It was just a touch, barely qualifying as a kiss, but this was Grayson. He could make her melt with a simple brush of his mouth and she'd forget all the arguments she had going through her head about why she couldn't do this. Kissing would only lead to more complications.

Still, Eve moved closer.

She hooked her arm around the back of his neck and eased him down to her. His mouth pressed harder, and that barely-a-kiss became a real one.

He snapped her to him, body to body, and took her mouth the way he always had. He was clever and thorough, and any thought of resisting him flew right out of her mind.

In fact, she did the opposite of resisting.

Eve got even closer, sliding her hands down his back and adjusting their positions so that the kiss turned to full body contact. Yes, there were clothes between them, but she knew his body so well that she had no trouble filling in the blanks of how it would feel to have him naked against her.

"You still can't?" he mumbled against his mouth.

She couldn't answer because the kiss turned French and scalding hot. If she'd had breath left to speak, she wouldn't have used it to state the obvious because clearly she *could*.

Couldn't she?

This wouldn't be lab sex for the purpose of getting her pregnant. This would be like old times. And then what?

Eve forced herself to consider *then what*.

Grayson cursed, and for a moment she thought he had reached the same *then what?* roadblock that she had. It took her a moment to realize he was cursing because his phone was ringing. She hadn't heard it over the roar in her head.

"It's Nate," Grayson let her know after he glanced down at the screen. He flipped the cell open and jabbed the speaker button. He also leaned against the kitchen counter and tried to level his breathing.

Eve did the same, though it would take more than some deep breaths to get back to normal.

"Please tell me you have good news," he greeted Nate.

"Well, it's news," Nate explained. "I'll let you decide if it's good or not. Just got the preliminary DNA results, and Nina Manning was indeed Sophia Collier."

So there it was—the proof that at least some of the Colliers weren't going to like because that proof was also motive.

"I did a statewide search of labs that had tested Sophia's DNA," Nate continued, "and I couldn't find any record that Cicely had requested a test."

Another lie, and Eve was betting that Cicely would just lie again when Grayson questioned her about it.

Eve huffed. Would they ever learn the truth so that Sophia's killer could be brought to justice and so that she could finally get on with her life?

She looked at Grayson and felt his kiss still burning her mouth. Maybe getting on with her life wasn't even possible. That kiss had proven that she would never get Grayson out of her blood and out of her system.

Never.

"But someone else did request a test on Sophia's DNA," Nate added. That caught Eve's attention. "That happened just three days before Sophia was murdered."

"Who?" Grayson and Eve asked in unison.

"Sebastian," Nate answered.

Eve saw the surprise in Grayson's eyes. Sebastian had denied that Nina was his sister, but yet he obviously knew the truth because he'd had her DNA tested.

"You're positive about this?" Grayson pressed.

"Positive, and I have proof. Sebastian tried to cover up the payment for the test by using cash, but the lab has 24/7 surveillance. We have footage of him going into the lab and then picking up the results."

"What kind of a timeline are we looking at for this? Did Sebastian have the DNA results before Nina was murdered?" Grayson wanted to know.

"Oh, yeah," Nate assured him. "He had them all right. Less than twenty-four hours after he got the results that confirmed Nina was his sister, someone killed her."

Grayson shook his head, mumbled something. "Then as far as I'm concerned, that makes Sebastian Collier our number-one suspect."

Eve agreed, and judging from the sound he made, apparently so did Nate.

"So what do you want me to do?" Nate asked Grayson.

Grayson didn't even hesitate. "Pick up Sebastian and put him in a holding cell. I'll be at SAPD first thing in the morning to read him his rights and arrest him."

Chapter 15

Grayson downed the shot of whiskey. It was strong stuff, Mason's private stash, and it burned his eyes and throat. What it didn't do was clear his head.

But then, that was asking a lot from a shot of whiskey.

The details of the case kept running through his head. Thoughts of Eve kept running through his body. Neither would give him much peace tonight, even though the house was whisper-quiet and would likely stay that way because it was going on midnight.

"Midnight," he mumbled.

Since he had an early-morning trip to SAPD to question and arrest Sebastian, he should be sleeping. Heck, Eve probably was. She'd called it a night well over an hour ago.

Good thing, too, because before her good-night Grayson had been on the verge of resuming the make-out session that Nate's call had interrupted.

He shouldn't have touched her.

And he damn sure shouldn't have kissed her.

He should have just walked away and let fate sort out the details of what was to come in the next week or so. But the sight of those tears in her eyes had shaken him. Grayson considered himself a strong man, but he wasn't strong enough to keep her at arm's length when she'd been crying.

He poured himself another shot and took it in one gulp. Still no relief. So he gave up on the whiskey and headed out of the den and to his bathroom for a shower. He stripped along the way, dropping his clothes on the bedroom floor, and he kept the water ice-cold.

That didn't work, either.

There was a furnace of heat in his body, and there was only one cure for what he felt.

Eve.

Damn her. Damn *him*.

Grayson knew that pretty much any woman

could satisfy his body, but there was only one woman who could satisfy *him*. And that was Eve.

For most of his life, she'd been what had fired him up and cooled him down—sometimes in the same minute. She'd been the one woman he couldn't get out of his head. And no amount of whiskey or cold water was going to cure that. No. There was only one cure, and she was right across the hall.

Grayson cursed and put on his jeans. No sense trying to talk himself out of jumping off this Texas-size cliff. He was going to jump all right, and this could be a fall that would hurt for the rest of his life.

He didn't knock on the guestroom door. Didn't want anything to slow him down and stop him. Well, that was the plan anyway, but his mouth went dry when he spotted her. Not asleep as he'd thought she would be. No. Eve was wide-awake, lying in bed, the ice-white covers draped loosely over her breasts and the rest of her.

Grayson shut the door. And went to her.

"The right thing would be for me to go back to my room," he told her.

Her mouth trembled slightly and turned into the hint of a smile. "Grayson, for once in your life, don't do the right thing, okay?"

She caught on to his hand, pulled him

closer. Grayson obliged and leaned down for a kiss. He'd kissed her a thousand times, maybe more, but each time always felt like the first. That punch hit him hard in the chest and then below the belt.

How could he want anyone this much?

And worse, why would he want her this much even after he'd had her?

Grayson kept the kiss simple, though his body was revved up way past the kissing stage. Still, he needed this. The feel of her mouth against his. The sweet silk of her lips. Her taste. He needed it all, and apparently Eve did, too, because she kept inching him closer.

The covers shifted, and the sheet slipped off her breasts. No bra. Just Eve's bare breasts. He met her gaze and saw the little spark there.

Grayson used just the tip of his index finger to draw the covers down. He got an interesting show as he revealed every inch of her. Bare stomach. Bare hips. He heard himself choke back a groan.

No panties.

"I like to sleep naked," she whispered.

"I like that you like to sleep naked." He tried to chuckle. Failed at that, too.

"No." Eve tightened the grip on his hand. "Don't you dare have any doubts about this."

Oh. He had doubts, but he wasn't going to

do anything about them. Grayson did what he did best. He took control of the situation. He raked back the rest of the covers, exposing every bit of Eve's naked body.

Yeah, she was beautiful.

He hadn't had to see her naked to remember that, but this trip down memory lane was a good one.

Grayson put his knee on the bed, the feather mattress giving way to his weight. He let himself ease into a fall and kissed her on the way down until his body was pressed hard against hers. The fit was right. Perfect. And it created pressure in all the right places.

"Jeans," she mumbled and fumbled for his zipper.

Grayson let her deal with that so he could make some headway with what he'd started. And what he'd started was a full-body kiss.

He trailed the kisses down her throat to her breasts. Yeah. That taste hadn't changed. He took her nipple into his mouth, and the zipper fumbling stopped, just as he figured it would. Eve moaned, arched her back and shoved her fingers into his hair to pull him closer.

"Yes." She repeated it and wrapped her legs around him.

His jeans were still between them, but Eve

got the position and the pressure just right for this to go to the next level.

"Make me crazy, Grayson," she whispered and then laughed, low and husky.

He was too involved in the kissing to laugh, but he smiled when he slid his body through her leg lock and kissed her where she really wanted to be kissed. Right in the center of all that wet heat.

But Eve didn't stay on just the receiving end. She ran her hands over his shoulder and into his hair. Her legs caressed his back...and lower.

She knew exactly how to drive him crazy, too. And how to pleasure him. After all, they'd spent their teen years making out in his truck. Kisses only, at first. Lots of kisses.

Then, the touches.

He'd given Eve her first climax with his hand in her panties. They'd lost their virginity on her seventeenth birthday. They'd both been clumsy and awkward. But they'd both learned a lot over the years.

"Too crazy," she let him know when she was close to climaxing.

She caught on to him, pulling him back up so she could go after his zipper again. She wasn't playing this time. She was hot and ready so Grayson helped her, and she used her feet and hands to work the jeans off his hips.

"Commando," she said when she noticed he wasn't wearing his usual boxers. She smiled when she looked down between their bodies and no doubt saw that he was hard as stone. "That's my Grayson."

She froze and got that deer-in-the-headlights look. As if she'd crossed some line and tried to take them back to a place they could never go again. And maybe she had with that *my Grayson*. But he didn't care a flying fig about lines. He'd crossed the biggest line of all just by coming into her room.

He pinned her hands to the bed. Pinned her body, too. She would want his full weight on her so Grayson obliged, and he pushed himself inside her.

Mercy.

The pleasure was blinding.

It was like coming home for Christmas.

Eve arched her back and pressed her head against the pillow. She rocked her hips into his, causing him to go deep and hard into her. He was probably too rough. That thought was just a flash, and soon he couldn't think at all.

He moved inside her. Faster. Harder. Deeper. Until she was so close to climax. Until everything was a blur.

Everything except Eve.

Everything inside him pinpointed on her. Just her. The primal ache clawed away at him. This need as old as man. The need to take and claim.

But there were other needs, too.

And it was that need that sent Grayson in search of a kiss. He wanted the taste of her in his mouth when he lost all reason. When she slipped over the edge.

Eve came in a flash, when Grayson was deep inside her, when his mouth took hers.

Grayson said her name. It came from a place deeper than the primal need that had brought them to this point.

Somewhere in his brain, it registered that this was going to complicate the hell out of things. But that was only a split-second thought. Eve's legs tightened around him. She pulled him closer, and her climax brought on his.

Grayson felt his body surrender. Felt that slam of pleasure that was beyond anything he ever deserved to feel. Something so perfect. So amazing.

So Eve.

Chapter 16

"You did what?" Grayson snapped to the person on the other end of the phone.

Eve thought the caller might be Nate, but she wasn't sure, and she couldn't tell from the conversation what Grayson was snapping about now. But there was no doubt, he was snapping.

Eve stared out the car window, sipped her coffee and debated—again—what she should say to Grayson once he had finished this call. Or if she should say anything. After all, he certainly hadn't volunteered much about coming to her bed for one of the most amazing nights of her life.

In fact, he had avoided the subject.

Of course, he'd been on the phone most of the morning and during the entire drive from the ranch to San Antonio. So that was his excuse, but she had to wonder, if it hadn't been for the calls, would he have come up with another reason for them not to talk?

"You're positive this isn't some kind of ruse so Sebastian can escape?" Grayson demanded.

Mercy, that didn't sound good, and she didn't think it was a good sign when Grayson turned off the interstate two exits before the one for SAPD headquarters. Grayson had been on his way to arrest Sebastian, but there had obviously been a change of plans.

"No," Grayson continued. Except that wasn't a bark or a snarl. He mumbled it. "Eve's with me. There wasn't anyone at the ranch to stay with her. The ranch hands have already left for their Christmas break."

Even though he practically mumbled that part, too, she heard the frustration. Grayson hadn't wanted her to come along when he questioned Sebastian. He'd wanted her tucked safely away at the ranch, but both Dade and Mason were still in town working the details of Nina's murder. Or rather Sophia Collier's murder. And with Bessie and the ranch hands off the grounds, Grayson had reluctantly brought her along to arrest and interrogate Sebastian.

Not the ideal way to spend Christmas Eve.

Of course, the danger was almost certainly over for her now that the photos she'd taken were in the hands of the authorities. Sebastian had no reason to kill her. Well, unless he was hell-bent on getting some kind of revenge because she'd inadvertently incriminated him, and now that he was in police custody, even that wasn't possible.

She hoped.

This could all be over soon, especially if Grayson managed to get a confession from Sebastian. Or if something hadn't gone wrong with his arrest. Judging from Grayson's sour expression and change of direction, that wasn't just possible but likely.

Grayson slapped his phone shut and took the turn for San Antonio Memorial Hospital.

Her heart dropped.

"Is someone hurt?" she asked and then held her breath.

He shook his head. "Claude's doctor doesn't think he'll last much longer so he requested the family's presence at Claude's bedside. That includes Sebastian."

Since Claude was critical, the doctor's request was reasonable, or at least it would have been if Sebastian weren't a murder suspect.

"An SAPD officer is escorting Sebastian," Grayson let her know. "They should arrive at the hospital any minute now."

And that explained why Grayson took the final turn toward San Antonio Memorial. It wasn't a large hospital but was in one of the more affluent neighborhoods of the city. No surprise about that, considering Claude was a millionaire many times over.

"Did Nate say if Claude was talking?" Eve asked.

"He's lucid." Grayson paused. "And he wants to see me."

Strange. Claude certainly hadn't wanted to see Grayson when he'd been ordered to SAPD headquarters. "Do you think he'll make a deathbed confession?"

Grayson's scowl deepened. "Maybe. But if he does, it'll probably be for one reason—not to tell the truth, but to save his son."

Of course. With Claude dying, it wouldn't matter if he confessed to a murder he didn't commit. But then, it was possible that he had indeed killed Sophia since there was no tangible proof that Claude knew she was his biological daughter. And even if he had known, he could have killed her when he realized she wasn't the darling little girl he wanted in his family.

There was no street parking, just a multi-level parking garage so Grayson drove in and looked for a spot. He took the first one available, at the back of the second level.

Grayson glanced around. So did Eve. And somewhere amid the glancing, their gazes collided.

There.

Eve saw it in his eyes then—the conversation he'd been avoiding all morning.

"Do I need to apologize?" Grayson tossed out there like a gauntlet.

She thought about her answer. "No. Do I?" She tossed that proverbial gauntlet right back at him.

He cursed, looked away and scrubbed his hand over his face. "I'm the one who went to your bed."

"And I could have said no," Eve reminded him.

But that was a lie. She'd never been able to say no to Grayson, and she wouldn't have started last night. Still, this had caused more tension between them, and that's the last thing they needed when they were within minutes of facing the Colliers.

And facing a possible pregnancy.

Eve certainly hadn't been thinking about getting pregnant when Grayson had climbed into bed with her. She'd been thinking about making love with him, but now that it was the morning after, she knew that last night had increased her chances of getting the baby she'd always wanted.

However, it hadn't helped her *relationship* with Grayson.

She could feel his uneasiness, and she had to do something to diffuse it.

"What happened between us doesn't have to mean anything," she settled for saying, but those words hurt. Because it sure as heck had meant something to her. It meant that Grayson had still wanted her enough to risk plenty by coming to her like that.

He looked at her, as if he might dispute her not-mean-anything offer, but he only shook his head. "We'll talk about this later."

Eve caught on to his arm when he started to bolt. "No need." That hurt, too, but she had to give Grayson an out. He'd done her a huge favor by having sex with her, and she didn't want him to feel guilty or tormented.

She leaned over and brushed a chaste kiss on his cheek. "I already know how you feel about fatherhood, about a lot of things." Eve had to take a deep breath before continuing.

"And I know when this investigation is over, your life can get back to normal."

Something flashed through his metal-gray eyes, and his face tightened. For a moment she thought they might have that blowup they'd been skirting around all morning. But he didn't toss out any more gauntlets or launch into an argument. He eased her hand off his arm and stepped from the car.

Eve could only sigh and do the same.

The garage wasn't just dank, it was cold, and Eve pulled her coat tighter against her. She had no scarf or gloves. She'd forgotten to pick those up when they'd been at her condo the day before, and women's clothing was in short supply at the Ryland ranch. Eve had made do with the gray pants and sweater that she'd packed, but she had been forced to wear the same red coat that had survived their trek through the woods.

Ahead of her, Grayson pulled the sides of his buckskin jacket together, as well. No festive red for him. He was wearing his usual jeans and dark shirt. Practically a uniform for him. He'd also worn his badge and shoulder holster, of course, which meant because he was armed, they would have to go through security inside.

She fell in step alongside Grayson as they

walked to the elevator that would take them into the hospital, but they didn't get far before Grayson stopped. He lifted his head and looked around, just as he'd done when he had first parked. She looked, too, but only saw the sea of cars in the dimly lit space.

"Is something wrong?" Eve asked.

Grayson didn't answer. He glanced around again and caught on to her to get her moving to the elevator. It was clear he was hurrying now, but Eve didn't know why.

"I got a bad feeling," Grayson mumbled.

That put her on full alert because she knew from experience that Grayson's instincts were usually right.

And they were.

The sound zinged through the garage. It wasn't a blast. Eve wasn't sure what it was until the window shattered on the car next to them. Then she knew.

Oh, God.

Someone had fired at them.

Grayson cursed and shoved Eve to the side between two parked cars. He followed, moving directly in front of her, and in the same motion, he drew his gun.

What the hell was happening now?

The danger to Eve should be over. Finished.

She was no longer a threat to Sophia's killer since her photos had gone public. Obviously, the shooter wasn't aware of that.

Because another shot came right at them.

Not a loud blast but more like a swish. That meant the gunman was using a weapon rigged with a silencer.

This had to be connected to Sophia's murder. They couldn't be that unlucky to now be the victims of a random attack. Maybe someone didn't want them hearing whatever deathbed confession Claude was likely to make. If so, then it was even more vital that Grayson speak to the dying man.

Grayson pushed Eve flat on the concrete floor and tried to pinpoint the origin of those two shots. He also tried to spot the gunman. There was no sign of anyone, but he thought maybe the shots had come from a black van on the other side of the parking lot. It wasn't a huge space, only about fifty feet across, but with the vehicles jammed together, there were plenty of places for a would-be killer to hide.

"Call Nate and tell him we need backup," Grayson told Eve. Without taking his attention off that black van, he grabbed his phone from his jacket pocket and handed it to her.

Another shot.

This one smacked into the headlight of the

car right next to them. The glass shattered, flying through the air, and Grayson had to duck down and shield his eyes.

Almost immediately, he heard footsteps.

Behind him, he also heard Eve call Nate and request assistance, but Grayson shut out what she was saying and concentrated on those footsteps. Someone was running, and he caught just a glimpse of that someone before they ducked out of sight.

The person was dressed head-to-toe in black and was wearing a black baseball cap that obstructed the shooter's face.

It could be anyone.

And that *anyone* ducked between two other vehicles—a white pickup truck and a red sports car.

"Nate's on the way," Eve relayed. "He said he'll seal off the exits to the garage and do a silent approach."

Good. He needed his brother because this situation could get more dangerous than it already was. If anyone came out of that elevator, the gunman would probably shoot to kill so there'd be no witnesses to this attack. Plus, someone driving into the garage could also become a target. Right now though Grayson's biggest concern was Eve, and getting her safely out of there.

He lifted his head a fraction and listened for any sound of movement or more footsteps. None on both counts. Just Eve's too-fast breathing, and she was mumbling something that sounded like a prayer. She was obviously terrified, and it didn't help that this was the third attempt to kill her. In fact, it was probably worse now because she might be pregnant.

But Grayson pushed that thought out of his mind.

He needed to focus, and he couldn't do that if he thought about the baby he'd possibly made with Eve.

The next shot got his full attention. It didn't slam into the car as the others had. This one was aimed at the ground, and it ripped through the concrete just a few feet in front of them. The shooter had obviously gotten himself in a better position to deliver a fatal shot.

Grayson needed to throw him off-kilter as much as he could. That wouldn't be easy since he only had his sidearm. There was extra ammunition in his car, but that was yards away and would be too dangerous to try to reach. That meant he had to make every shot count while maneuvering the gunman as far away from Eve as possible.

Grayson waited for the next shot, and he

didn't have to wait long. It, too, tore into the floor and sent a cloud of debris and dangerous concrete bits right at them. He ducked out of cover for just a second and then fired in the direction of the shooter.

He hit the red sports car.

The shot bashed into the front end, and almost immediately the alarm went off. It was a piercing roar that was almost deafening. And worse. It blocked out any sound of the gunman's footsteps.

"Stay down!" Grayson warned Eve when he felt her move behind him.

He knew for a fact that she didn't have her gun with her because he'd talked her out of bringing it. Now, he wished he hadn't. He didn't want Eve up and returning fire, but it would have been nice to have the extra ammunition.

Even with the distraction of the car alarm, Grayson saw where the next shot landed. This one hadn't been aimed at them but rather the overhead lights. The gunman took out the ones near the elevator and stairwell, plunging that area into total darkness.

That could be good or bad.

Good because Nate would likely make his approach using the stairs, and the darkness would help conceal him. But that same darkness could also conceal the shooter if he tried to escape. Grayson didn't want this SOB to get away. He wanted to end this now.

Two more shots came at Eve and him, one right behind the other.

The gunman had moved again. This time to the right. Hell. The gunman was moving toward those stairs. Not only would that give him an escape route, it would also give him a better angle to fire more of those lethal bullets.

"What's going on up there?" someone called out. "I'm the security guard for the hospital."

"Sheriff Grayson Ryland. We're under fire. Stay back!"

But the words had no sooner left Grayson's mouth when he saw something out of the corner of his eye. To his left. There was a man in a dark gray uniform. The security guard, no doubt. He had his weapon drawn and had ducked down a little, but he was still making his way toward them.

The gunman obviously saw him, too.

Because a shot went in that direction.

The guard dove to the ground, but he was literally out in the open and therefore an easy target. Grayson had to do something, so he came out of cover, estimated the position of the shooter, and sent a bullet his way.

Because of the blasted car alarm, he couldn't tell if the gunman even reacted. Maybe he'd managed to hit the bastard, or at the very least maybe he had gotten the guy to back off so the guard could scramble to safety.

"You need to get down!" Eve snarled, and she put her hand on his back to push Grayson to the ground again.

It wasn't a second too soon.

The next bullet that was fired would have slammed right into him if Eve hadn't pulled him down with her.

However, Grayson didn't have time to thank her because everything seemed to happen at once. Another shot went toward the security guard who was trying to scramble away.

And then there was the movement in the stairwell.

For one horrifying moment, Grayson thought it was the gunman getting away. But this person wasn't dressed all in black.

It was Nate.

His brother was sneaking up the stairs, trying to get a drop on the gunman. But it was dark, and Nate was out of position. Unlike the gunman, who was probably only a few feet away.

"Watch out!" Grayson yelled to his brother.

But it was already too late.

Grayson couldn't hear the shot that the gunman fired, but he saw the end result.

A bullet slammed right into Nate's chest.

Chapter 17

Eve screamed, but the sound of her voice was drowned out by the blaring car alarm.

Her scream didn't warn Nate in time. Neither did Grayson's shouted warning to his brother. And because they'd failed, she watched in horror as the bullet hit Nate.

He flew backward from the impact.

"Oh, God." And Eve kept repeating it like a hysterical mantra.

Had he been killed?

She thought of his baby daughter, Kimmie, who would be an orphan if Nate died. And it would be partly her fault. If she just hadn't taken that damn picture then there would have been no attempts to kill her. All of this had started because of that.

Eve automatically bolted toward Nate so she could help him, but Grayson latched onto her and pulled her back to the ground. Good thing, too. Because the shots came at them again. This time, however, they were nonstop. Frenzied. They pelted into the cars on either side of them and the concrete floor in front of them.

Eve covered her head with her hands, but she couldn't stay behind the shelter of the vehicles for long. "We have to help Nate," she shouted, though she was certain that Grayson already knew that.

Because Grayson was practically lying on top of her, she could feel the rock-hard muscles of his body, and his chest was pumping from the adrenaline. His gaze volleyed between the stairwell and the area where the gunman was likely hiding. He was primed and ready to fight, but he would also do whatever it took to save his brother.

Eve couldn't see Nate, nor could she hear him, but she prayed he'd somehow managed to survive the gunshot and the fall. Either could have been fatal.

She saw some movement at the other end of the parking lot and spotted another uniformed security guard on the stairwell. He had his gun

ready, thank God, but he didn't seem to be in
any better position than Grayson was to stop
this. Still, he might be able to do some good
if the shooter moved.

Finally, the shots stopped. Maybe because
the gunman had to reload. Or, God forbid,
maybe because he was escaping. The thought
of that sickened Eve. She didn't want a killer
to get away.

But right now, Nate was their first priority.

Grayson eased off her and inched toward
the car to their right. He was probably thinking of making a run to the stairs, but she
prayed he wouldn't do that. He could end up
like Nate, or worse.

Since she still had Grayson's phone, she
called nine-one-one to report an officer down,
though someone was likely already aware of
that. She doubted that Nate had come alone.
But she immediately rethought that. Maybe
that's exactly what Nate had done. Maybe he'd
rushed to help his brother and her and hadn't
considered the consequences.

She would have reacted the same way if it
meant saving Grayson.

The moment she ended the call, Eve saw
Grayson's gaze swing to the left. And she soon
saw why. The first security guard was crawling toward them. She saw the blood on his

shoulder and knew that he, too, had been shot. They had to get an ambulance up here right away, but that couldn't happen until the gunman had been stopped.

Grayson latched on to the guard and pulled him next to Eve. The man was clearly in pain, and even though he was clutching his gun, he had both it and his hand pressed to the wound. It didn't take medical training to know he'd already lost too much blood. Eve pushed aside his hand so she could apply some pressure.

"Wait here," Grayson ordered. "Use the gun if you have to." His eyes met hers, and she could see that it was indeed an order.

But, God, what was he going to do?

Please.

She didn't want him out there in the open, making himself an easy target. She wanted him to stay behind cover, even though cover didn't mean safety. Not with those bullets flying everywhere.

Her heart was pounding against her chest now, and her breath was so thin that she felt light-headed. Despite the cold, there was a fine mist of clammy sweat on her face. She felt sick, but she tried to fight off the feeling of dread. They would survive this, somehow, because there was no other alternative. It couldn't end here for Grayson and Nate.

Grayson took the gun from the security guard and handed it to her. Eve latched on to it, but she was shaking her head. "You can't go out there."

He shook his head, too. "I don't have a choice. This has to stop."

That was it. No other explanation. Grayson maneuvered around her and the guard and went behind them. He disappeared when he ducked around the front of the car to her right.

Well, at least he wasn't going to charge out into the center of the garage. He was obviously trying to get to the stairwell, and maybe the security guard could provide some backup. However, that still meant Grayson was moving closer and closer to the gunman, and she was betting the gunman would be looking for them to do just that. Shooting Nate could have all been designed to draw Grayson and her out into the open.

If so, it had worked.

Eve couldn't hear what the security guard was mumbling, but he squirmed, his face tightening in pain. She pressed harder on the wound to try to stop the flow of blood, but she also kept watch of the area near the black van where the last shots had originated.

"This is Sergeant O'Malley, SAPD." The man's voice boomed from a bullhorn. It sounded as if he was at street level. "Put down your weapon and surrender."

Backup. Thank God. But since there was no response from the shooter, Eve doubted he would just do as the sergeant had demanded.

By her calculations it'd been a minute, maybe more, and the gunman hadn't fired. Eve had no idea if that was good or bad, but it was certainly easier to think without those bullets bashing into the cement and other cars.

And because it was easier to think, tears sprang to her eyes.

Eve blinked them back. She couldn't give in to the worry and fear, but she was terrified for Grayson. For Nate. For this wounded security guard whom she didn't even know.

But who was out there doing this?

Sebastian? Maybe. But only if he'd managed to get away from his police escort. Of course, either Claude or Sebastian could have hired a gunman. It was possible Claude wasn't even in critical condition but instead had orchestrated this to get Grayson and her into a position so they could be killed.

That brought her back to why again.

If they could just figure out who'd fired shots at them, then knowing the *who* would tell them the *why*.

Eve finally spotted Grayson again. He was

seven cars over to her right and was inching his way to the stairwell. She held her breath, waiting for another shot.

Nothing.

The seconds crawled by so slowly that she could feel them ticking off in her head. Finally, she saw some movement in the stairwell.

Nate.

Thank God he was moving. However, he wasn't just moving. He had his gun aimed and ready and was making his way back up the stairs. Not easily. He, too, was wincing, and Eve soon realized why. His shirt was open, but there was no blood. Only a Kevlar vest.

Relieved, she let out her breath in a rush. Nate hadn't been shot. The impact of the bullet had probably knocked him down the stairs. He looked shaken up but very much alive.

So that was one prayer that'd been answered.

The security guard moved again, the muscles in his body going stiff, and Eve looked down at him to see what had caused that reaction. His eyes were wide and not focused on her.

But rather behind her.

Oh, God.

That was the only thought that had time to form in her head because Eve felt a hand grip on to her shoulder. She didn't have time to move. There was no time to react.

Before someone pressed the barrel of a gun to her head.

Grayson's heart went to his knees.

This couldn't be happening.

He'd had just a split second of relief because his brother was alive, but that relief went south in a hurry when he saw Eve. She was no longer where Grayson had left her—crouched with the injured security guard between the two cars. She was standing now.

And she wasn't alone.

Someone was behind her, their arm curved around Eve's neck, and that someone had a gun pointed directly at Eve's head. The person had a second gun next to Eve's neck. Both weapons were positioned to deliver a fatal shot.

Grayson couldn't see the person's face, only the black baseball cap. But he could see Eve's. The color had drained from her cheeks, and she was looking around as if trying to figure out how to escape.

But Grayson didn't want her to move.

Not with that gun pressed to her head.

"Drop your weapon and surrender," Sergeant O'Malley called out again.

Grayson was thankful for the backup, but he didn't want the sergeant's demand to make this bad situation worse.

He took aim, and with his attention nailed to the gunman's hand, Grayson inched closer.

"There's no need to do this," Grayson shouted. "Let her go."

If the gunman responded, Grayson didn't hear it. He wished like the devil that the car alarm would stop. He had to try to negotiate Eve's release, and it was hard to do that when he couldn't hear what was going on.

"Eve is no threat to you," Grayson tried again, all the while moving closer.

He didn't have a clean shot, not with the gunman using Eve as a human shield, but he needed to get as close as possible because it was likely this SOB was planning an escape. After all, Eve was still alive, and there had to be a reason for that. The gunman had taken her hostage.

But why?

Grayson was certain he would soon learn the answer, but he hoped he wouldn't learn it too late. Eve couldn't die. She just couldn't. Someway, somehow, he had to put himself in a position where he could save her.

He glanced over his shoulder at his brother. Nate wasn't following him but instead had crouched down and was making his way to the other side of the garage toward the black van and the red car with the blaring alarm.

Good move.

His brother might get a better angle on a shot that way, and Nate could also possibly block an attempted escape. The second security guard could help with that, too, since he was covering the other end of the garage. Grayson couldn't let the gunman get Eve out of there because once he no longer had any use for a hostage, the shooter would almost certainly kill her.

"The security guard needs medical attention," Grayson shouted to the gunman. Since the guy wasn't moving, he wanted to try a different approach. "Why don't you end this now so we can get an ambulance up here?"

Still nothing. But the guy was moving a little and looking around. Grayson didn't like the edgy movement because it proved the gunman was nervous and way out of his comfort zone.

Grayson stopped but kept his gun lifted and aimed. "Step out so I can see you." And he tried to make it sound like an order. Hard to do with that gun right at Eve's head.

"What should I do?" she mouthed.

But Grayson shook his head. He didn't want her to do anything. Not yet anyway. But if it came down to it, he hoped she could drop out of the way so that Nate or he would have a clean shot.

Grayson glanced around to see the best way to approach this, and while he was still studying the situation, just like that the car alarm stopped. Maybe the battery had given out or perhaps Nate had managed to disarm it. Either way, it was now deadly silent.

The gunman lifted his head, just a little, and even though Grayson still couldn't see his face, he didn't think it was his imagination that the guy wasn't pleased with the silenced alarm. But Grayson was certainly thankful for it. Maybe now he could hear this bozo's voice and figure out who he was dealing with. If it wasn't Sebastian, then maybe one of the Colliers had hired a triggerman.

"SAPD has the building surrounded," Grayson tossed out there. "You can't escape. But what you can do is let Eve go, and we can talk about a peaceful surrender."

No answer, but he hadn't expected one.

The guy finally moved. Well, he moved the gun away from Eve's head anyway, and for a moment Grayson thought he might surrender. He didn't.

He lowered the gun, pointing it down to the floor, and he fired.

Hell.

Grayson couldn't see exactly what had happened, but judging from the look of sheer horror on Eve's face and from her scream, the gunman had shot the security guard at point-blank range.

Things had just gone from bad to worse.

The gunman moved again, quickly this time. He put the gun back against Eve's head and he pushed her forward. He followed with the front of his body pressed to Eve's back.

The gunman was heading for that black van.

Nate was there, somewhere. Hopefully, in a position to stop a getaway attempt.

"You won't be able to drive out of here," Grayson warned.

But he'd barely had time to issue that warning when the gunman shifted his weapon.

He fired at Grayson.

Grayson jumped to the side, just in time, and he landed hard against the concrete floor. His shoulder jammed, the pain shooting through him, but he ignored it and came up ready to fire.

The gunman fired first, and the shot pinned Grayson down behind the back of a small truck.

"I have to kill you, you know," the gunman said.

Or rather the gunwoman. Because that was a female voice. A familiar one.

"Cicely?" Grayson spat out. She was the last of the Colliers that he had suspected. "Why the hell are you doing this?"

"Because you all have to die." Cicely's voice was eerily calm, but there was nothing calm about her expression when she met his gaze over Eve's shoulder. "Step out and die like a man, Sheriff Ryland. The other one, too." She tossed a look in Nate's direction. "And that other security guard."

She was just going to kill them all?

Why?

"Your son is in custody for Sophia's murder," Grayson tossed out there. He was testing the waters, trying to get Cicely to talk. And he was also hoping to distract her.

What he didn't intend to do was surrender.

"That's a mistake. He didn't kill his sister." Cicely's voice broke on the last word. "I know because I did it."

Eve gasped, and that was pretty much Grayson's reaction. "You killed your own daughter?"

A hoarse sob tore from Cicely's mouth. "It was an accident, but I don't expect you to believe that."

"I do." And Grayson wasn't lying. He did believe her. "Why did you do it?"

With Eve still in a body lock against her, Cicely continued to inch toward the black van. "I'll tell you, but it won't save you. Nothing will."

Grayson would prove her wrong, somehow.

"I begged Sophia to come home to me, but she just laughed. She wanted money, you see. Claude's money and mine. She didn't want us. Didn't want to be family again."

"So you killed her?" Eve asked in disbelief.

Cicely jammed the gun harder against Eve's head. "I told you that was an accident," Cicely practically yelled. "Sophia said her foster mother confessed to her who she really was—a Collier. The foster mother wanted to try and get money out of us. But Sophia gave her an overdose of insulin to get her out of the way."

Grayson didn't think Sophia's motives were pure, that she did that in order to protect her biological parents. "Sophia did that so she wouldn't have to share the cash with her foster mother?" he asked.

Cicely nodded. "Then, when Sophia and I were arguing, I pushed her, and she fell and hit her head." Another sob. "I had Leon dispose of the body. But Leon remembered that someone at the rodeo had been taking pictures. Pictures that would link him to Sophia. And eventually link her back to me. Leon tried to get them back from Eve, and then you killed him."

"Because he tried to kill us," Grayson reminded her. "Eve did nothing wrong. She was only doing her job when she took the pictures."

"Yes, but I couldn't have the police thinking Sebastian had anything to do with this. He's innocent, you know." She pulled in a shaky breath. "Now step out, Sheriff, and drop your gun so I can do what I have to do to protect my son."

"You mean so you can kill me," he answered flatly.

Eve frantically shook her head. "Stay put," she told Grayson.

Cicely fired at shot at him. "If you stay put or hold on to your gun, I'll make it painful for Eve. You're not the sort of man to cower behind a car while the woman you love is screaming in pain."

Grayson ignored that *woman you love* part and got ready to move. He would leave cover. There was no question about that. He wouldn't let this insane woman hurt Eve. But he couldn't just let Cicely kill him either, because he had to live so that he could rescue Eve. He wouldn't do her any good if he was dead.

"I'm coming out," Grayson let Cicely know. He glanced over at Nate who was ready to fire, as well.

Grayson slid out his gun first, not too far away. He needed to be able to reach for it. And then he stood.

At the exact moment that Eve shouted, "No!"

Eve rammed her elbow against Cicely and darted to the side. But Grayson didn't have time to get off a clean shot. Because Cicely darted to the side, too, and the woman didn't release the grip she had on Eve.

Grayson yelled for Eve to get out of the way, but the sound he heard turned his blood to ice.

The sound of the shot that Cicely fired.

Not at Grayson. Nor at Nate.

Grayson's world tipped on its axis when the bullet slammed into Eve.

Chapter 18

Eve heard the shot.

She also heard Grayson call out to her.

But she couldn't answer. She couldn't do anything except slide to the floor.

The pain was instant, searing, and it sliced through her right side like a red-hot stiletto. She grabbed at the fire and felt the warm blood against her fingers.

She'd been shot.

That fact registered somewhere in her mind. It also registered that she needed to tell Grayson to get down so that he, too, wouldn't be shot. But Eve couldn't make herself speak.

Was she in shock?

Or worse, was she dying?

Ironically, she could deal with the thought of her death, but not of Grayson's. She didn't want his life to end here in this cold, dank garage.

Because she was in love with him.

Always had been. Always would be.

And that's why she had to save him. At least one of them had to make it out of here alive.

"Eve?" Grayson called out. "Are you all right?"

She tried to answer, but Cicely was still beside her, crouched down, with a gun in each hand. She jammed the gun to Eve's head again.

"Tell him to come to you," Cicely demanded.

Eve shook her head. She had to do something to buy a little time. "They'll put you in jail," she managed to say to the woman who'd just shot her. "They'll give you the death penalty. All of this will be for nothing."

"No," Cicely quickly disagreed. Her eyes were wild, her gaze firing between Grayson and Nate. "Annabel is tied up in that black van. When the Rylands and you are dead, I'll shoot her and make it look like a suicide. I've already forced her to write the note, and trust me, it'll be no hardship killing that bimbo witch. She stole my husband. And my life. She deserves to die a thousand deaths."

Oh, God. Cicely wasn't just crazy, she was smart. If Eve couldn't fight back and stop her, Cicely might just get away with this. Worse, Cicely was trying to maneuver herself into a better position to kill again.

Cicely tucked the gun she'd been holding in her left hand into the waist of her pants. That meant she could use that hand to put a tight grip around Eve's neck. Cicely wasn't choking her, exactly, but it was close. Eve was already light-headed enough, but it was obvious Cicely was going to do anything to force Eve to cooperate.

"Tell the sheriff to come to you," Cicely repeated. "And make sure he's unarmed."

She would die before she did that because Cicely intended to kill them all anyway. Eve wouldn't be the reason Grayson took a bullet.

"You're not just killing me," Eve whispered. "I'm pregnant. You're killing my child, too. Maybe a daughter. It would be like killing Sophia all over again."

Cicely blinked, and with that blink Eve saw the hesitation in the woman's eyes. Her gaze dropped to Eve's stomach and then to the blood on the side of Eve's gray sweater. It wasn't much more than a split second of time, but that brief lapse was all that Eve needed.

She latched on to Cicely's wrist.

It was risky, but at this point anything she did or didn't do was risky. All she knew was that every drop of blood she lost put Grayson, Nate, her possible pregnancy and herself in danger. Besides, Cicely had killed both Sophia and the security guard, and Eve knew she wouldn't hesitate to kill again.

Cicely made a feral sound, part scream and part groan, and she struggled to throw off Eve's grip. Eve held on and tried to wrench the gun from Cicely's right hand. Of course, the woman had a second gun that she could use, but Eve would deal with that later. For now, she needed a weapon so she could fight back.

"Eve?" Grayson called out.

The sound of the struggle must have alerted him because Eve heard his frantic footsteps. He was running to try and save her.

Or maybe running to his death.

Eve clamped onto Cicely's gun because she knew that Grayson's life depended on it.

Grayson cursed, and even though Eve couldn't see him from her position, he was close by. Cicely was aware of that, too, because she bashed the gun against Eve's head and then pointed the weapon at Grayson.

Cicely fired.

The fear and adrenaline slammed through

Eve, and despite the blow Cicely had delivered
to her head, she kept fighting.

"Grayson!" Nate called out.

Nate sounded terrified, and that spiked the
fear inside Eve. Did that mean he'd just witnessed his brother being shot?

Oh, God.

Eve couldn't risk thinking about that now.
She had to stay in the fight. Despite the pain
and the fear, she had to keep fighting.

"Come closer and he dies," she heard Cicely say, and she let go of Eve.

Eve swiveled around and realized Cicely
was talking to Nate as he approached them.
He had obviously retrieved his weapon and
now had it trained on Cicely.

But Cicely had her gun aimed at Grayson.

Another smart move because Nate wouldn't
do anything to risk his brother being killed.

Nate froze, but he didn't lower his gun, and
he glanced behind him at the stairwell. Hopefully, there were backup officers there and
ready to respond.

And then there was Grayson.

He, too, was ready to respond, but he was
no longer the calm, collected lawman. Grayson said her name.

Eve.

It was a hoarse whisper filled with concern. No doubt from the blood.

"I'm okay," Eve said to him, even though she had no idea if that was true. She might have lost the chance to be a mother, but worse, she might lose Grayson. "I'm so sorry," she managed to say.

He shook his head. "For what?"

Too many things for her to say here. Besides, there was nothing she could say that would allow them to go back and undo everything. This was their fate, and unfortunately it was in the hands of a crazy woman hellbent on covering up the murder of her own daughter.

"Eve needs a doctor," Grayson told Cicely. "End this now."

"It ends when you're all dead." But Cicely didn't sound as convinced of that as she had just moments earlier. She glanced at Eve. "I didn't know about your baby. If I had, I would have found a way to leave you out of this."

"Baby?" Nate mumbled. That obviously shocked him, but he didn't take his attention off Cicely.

Later, Eve would have to explain.

If there was a later.

The pain shot through her side again, and Eve felt the fresh trickle of warm blood. Gray-

234 *Grayson*

son noticed it, too, because she saw his body tense. He was getting ready to have a shoot-out with Cicely. And he could no doubt kill her. But could he do that before she fired a lethal shot at him?

Eve couldn't take that risk. She had to do something, and she used her own body. She kicked at Cicely, and she put every ounce of her strength behind it. The heel of her shoe connected with the woman's shin, and Cicely howled in pain.

It wasn't much of an attack, but Grayson made the most of it.

He dove at Cicely, his muscled body ramming right into the woman, and he slammed her back into the adjacent car.

Cicely made a gasping sound, fighting for the air that Grayson had knocked from her, but that didn't stop her from trying to aim her gun at his head.

"Watch out!" Eve shouted.

Grayson latched on to both of Cicely's hands and bashed them against the car's body. Her gun clattered to the floor, and Grayson snatched the other weapon from the waist of her pants. He tossed it on the floor, as well.

Nate moved in and kicked both of Cicely's weapons away, but even unarmed, Cicely didn't give up. She continued to fight until

Grayson turned her around and pushed her hard against the car's fender.

A sob racked through Cicely, and she went limp.

"Take Cicely," Grayson immediately told Nate. "I'm getting Eve to the E.R."

He kept his forearm on Cicely to hold her until Nate switched places with him. Grayson didn't waste a second. He scooped Eve up in his arms.

"How bad?" he asked.

She wanted to lie. Eve wanted to tell him that everything would be all right, but the fight had taken the last of her breath. She opened her mouth, but no sound came out.

Grayson raced to the stairwell where the other officers were pouring up the steps. One of those officers latched onto Cicely, yanked her hands behind her back and cuffed her.

Grayson looked down at Eve as he ran toward the E.R. doors. He was so worried. And scared. She realized that was the first time she'd seen fear in Grayson's eyes.

Everything started to move in slow motion, and the edges of her vision turned gray. At first. Then, darker.

She fastened her gaze on Grayson and fought to keep her eyes open. But she failed at that, too.

Her eyelids fluttered down, and the last thing Eve saw was Grayson's face.

Grayson was afraid if he stopped moving, he would explode.

So he turned and once again paced across the surgical waiting room of the San Antonio hospital. It didn't help his raw nerves, nor did it ease the massive knot in his stomach, but he couldn't sit and wait as his brothers were doing.

Nate and Dade were on the far side of the room. Nate was on the phone, but both Dade and he were staring at a TV where *It's a Wonderful Life* was playing. Grayson doubted they were actually watching the movie, but they were trying to maintain a calm, business-as-usual facade. For his sake no doubt.

They knew he was ready to explode.

Mason, being Mason, didn't even attempt a facade. He was in a chair on the opposite side of the room, and he was glaring at anything and everything—including Jimmy Stewart on the screen. He was especially glaring at the hall where a nurse had appeared earlier to tell them that Eve was finally being taken to surgery.

Two hours.

That's how long it'd been since Eve had

been in the hospital. Grayson hadn't known that one hundred and twenty minutes could feel like a lifetime, but he damn sure knew it now. Every one of those minutes had crawled by.

"She'll be okay," Nate assured him.

Dade mumbled his agreement, but it didn't sound remotely convincing. Mason's glare deepened.

The glare wasn't for Eve. Mason wasn't fond of too many people, but he cared as much for Eve as Grayson's other brothers did. No, this glare was for Cicely, for what the woman had nearly done to Eve. But the good thing in all of this was that Cicely was locked away at the SAPD facility and couldn't come after any of them again.

"Claude Collier's condition has stabilized," Nate reported when he ended the call. "Annabel's still being checked out over in the E.R., but she's going to be okay. Just some bruises and scratches from where Cicely attacked her and stuffed her in the van."

It was the wrong attitude for a lawman to have, but Grayson didn't give a flying fig about the Colliers. He only wanted good news about Eve.

At the sound of footsteps in the hall, his brothers stood, and Grayson turned to see Dr.

Andrew Masters making his way toward him. Grayson had met the lanky no-nonsense doctor briefly when Eve had first been rushed into the E.R.

Grayson narrowed the distance between the doctor and him. "Is she okay?" he asked. But he wasn't sure he could take hearing any bad news.

The doctor nodded. "Eve should be fine."

"Should be?" Mason growled, taking the tone and the words right out of Grayson's mouth. "What the hell does that mean?"

The doctor gave a weary huff and looked at Grayson. "Physically, she'll be all right. The surgery didn't take long at all."

"Then what did?" That growl came from Dade. "It's been two hours."

"She had to be examined and prepped. The bullet entered her right side and made a clean exit. It didn't hit any vital organs, which makes her a very lucky woman."

Lucky. Yes, she was, but Grayson didn't feel so lucky. Eve had come damn close to dying.

"You said *physically* Eve will be all right?" Nate questioned.

Dr. Masters glanced at Grayson. A funny kind of glance. Had Eve told him about the possible pregnancy?

No doubt.

She might not have actually mentioned that Grayson could be her baby's father, but the doctor wasn't an idiot. He had almost certainly put one and one together when he's seen Grayson's reaction to her being shot.

"Eve wants to see you," the doctor said to Grayson. "But don't stay long. I want her to get plenty of rest." Then, he turned that authoritative gaze on the rest of the Rylands. "You can all come back in the morning."

The trio looked as if they might argue, but Nate finally caught on to his brothers' arms. "Grayson will see to Eve," he reminded them.

Yeah. He'd done a stellar job of that in the past forty-eight hours, hadn't he? He'd had sex with her, twice, and had nearly gotten her killed.

Grayson took a deep breath and followed the doctor to the post-op room at the end of the hall. Everything in the room was watery white, including Eve. There wasn't a drop of color in her cheeks. Still, she managed a smile of sorts when she saw him.

"You've got five minutes," the doctor instructed, "and then I don't want her to have any more visitors until tomorrow. Don't worry. After what Eve's been through, she'll sleep during that time anyway."

Grayson prayed that was true, that she

would sleep with no nightmares. He stood zero chance of that happening for him. Every time he closed his eyes, he would see the attack. It would torment him, and he would try to figure out what he could have done to prevent it. In his nightmares, he would stop Cicely's bullet from hitting Eve.

But saving her from that bullet was a day late and a dollar short.

"You look worried," she mumbled. Her words were slurred, and her eyes bleary.

"I am worried." Grayson walked closer. She looked too fragile to touch, but he skimmed his fingers down her arm, barely making contact with her skin. "The doctor said you were going to be okay."

"Yes." The half smile faded. "It's too early to know if that's true."

"The baby," he whispered.

She gave a shaky nod. "The trauma probably put an end to any pregnancy."

Of course. Her body had been through a lot. Too much. He didn't know much about the biology of conception, but the blood loss and the shock from the attack could have caused her body to shut down.

Being shot was hardly conducive to making a baby.

"Dr. Masters said I should brace myself for

the worst," she added. "So that's what I've done."

It made him ache to hear her say that, to see the resignation in her exhausted eyes.

"I'm sorry," Grayson said, because he didn't know what else to say.

She lifted her chin, though it was shaky, too. "I just wanted to thank you, for everything. That's why I asked to see you."

That hurt, as well. And it also riled him to the core. Grayson didn't want to be thanked for doing a half-assed job at protecting her. "Don't—"

"I know. You don't want to talk about it." She pulled in a slow breath and fought to keep her eyes open. "That's okay."

No. It wasn't *okay*. Far from it. He should tell her…

But tell her what, exactly?

Tell her that he wasn't sorry about sleeping with her? That was a moot point now that the gunshot wound had compromised her already slim chances of getting pregnant.

Maybe he should explain to her that he was sorry he hadn't stopped Cicely from shooting her? Or that the only thing he wanted was for her to be happy? She deserved happiness. She deserved a lot more than he could have ever given her.

But Grayson didn't say any of those things. He just stood there, looking at Eve, and knowing he couldn't do or say anything to make it better.

"Go home to your family." Her voice had no sound now. Even though her eyes drifted down, she smiled that sad half smile again. "Have a good life, Grayson."

The words went through him like ice. Like the dark cold he felt deep within his soul when he thought he'd lost Eve in that parking garage.

Because the words sounded like a goodbye.

And Grayson knew that's exactly what it was.

Well, he had his answer. Eve might have been groggy from the surgical drugs, but he hadn't seen any doubt in her eyes, and she damn sure hadn't asked him to stay.

Have a good life, Grayson.

With those words slamming through his head, Grayson did as Eve wanted. He walked away.

Chapter 19

The pain seared through her when she eased off the hospital bed and into the wheelchair, but Eve tried not to react visibly. She didn't want Dr. Masters to see the pain on her face because he would only give her more hassle about leaving. And there was no way she wanted to spend the rest of Christmas day in a hospital.

Besides, if she stayed, she would go stark-raving mad. Every moment she was in that bed, she thought of Grayson and of the life that she'd nearly gotten to have as a mother.

"You know how I feel about this," the doctor grumbled. It was a paraphrase of the grumble he'd been doling out since she'd insisted on going home.

So yes, she did know how the doctor felt. He wanted her to stay put one more day, even at the risk of her sanity. However, the moment he signed the release papers, Eve snatched them from his hand.

Dr. Masters gave her a flat look. "At least tell me you'll be with family or friends, that you aren't going home alone."

"I won't be alone," she lied.

His flat look intensified. "You told the nurse to tell the Rylands that you couldn't have any visitors, that you were in too much pain."

"I lied about that." And that was the truth.

She had told that lie not because of the pain. Well, not the physical pain anyway, but she couldn't bear the thought of saying goodbye to Grayson again. Once she was home and had recovered, she would email his brothers and thank them for, well, for being there when it counted most.

Dr. Masters scribbled something on another piece of paper and handed it to her. "A script for pain meds and antibiotics," he explained.

The antibiotics were a necessity but not the drug for pain. The pain was right there, stabbing through her, but she didn't want to put any more drugs in her body in case there was the minuscule chance that she might be pregnant.

Yes, it was a pipe dream, but Eve was going

to hold on to it until a pregnancy test proved otherwise.

"I can't talk you out of this?" the doctor asked. He grabbed the back of her wheelchair when Eve tried to wheel herself toward the door.

"No. I've made up my mind."

He gave a heavy sigh, followed by a nod, and he stepped behind her so he could wheel her toward the door. With any luck, the taxi she'd called would be waiting and could take her to her condo. She'd also phoned the super because she didn't have her keys. He had promised to meet her there and let her in. Then she could get some cash to pay the taxi driver.

"What should I tell the Rylands when they show up?" Dr. Masters asked.

And they would show up. "Tell them I made a miraculous recovery and that I'm spending the holiday with friends."

The doctor made a sound of disapproval but wheeled her out anyway.

"The taxi is meeting me at the back of the building," she let him know.

Another sound of disapproval, but he went in that direction anyway. Eve looked over her shoulder. No sign of Grayson. And she tried to convince herself that was a good thing.

The tears came anyway.

She blinked them back and realized that the pain in her side was nothing compared to the piercing ache in her heart. Damn her. She had known not to get too close to Grayson, and she'd done it anyway.

Again.

The doors slid open as they approached, and the cold wind nearly robbed her of her breath. So did the man who stepped out onto the walkway. Not Grayson.

Dade.

He was there, right next to the taxi that was waiting for her. Dade smiled, flashing those killer dimples that had probably coaxed many women into his bed. The dimples had never worked on Eve because to her Dade would always be the brother she'd never had.

"I asked at the front desk," Dade explained, "and the nurse said you were checking out early. Since I didn't see you out front, I figured I'd check back here." He tipped his head to the taxi. "Going somewhere?" It was a friendly enough question, but there was concern in his voice.

"I need to get home." Eve kept it at that. She gave the doctor a nod of reassurance that all was well, and he went back inside.

"Right. You need to get home," Dade repeated. He blew out his breath as if resigned to the fact that they weren't going to have a real discussion here. "Want me to drive you?"

She shook her head. "It's Christmas and you should be with your family. The taxi will get me home just fine."

Another nod. He reached in his jeans' pocket, pulled out something and walked closer. "Your Christmas present," he announced. "Sorry, but I didn't have time to wrap it." Dade caught on to her hand and dropped something into her palm.

A silver concho.

Eve knew exactly what this was. One of the silver conchos that Boone Ryland had given to all six of his sons before he'd walked out on them and their mother.

She looked at Dade and shook her head. "I thought you threw yours in the creek."

Dade shrugged. "I had this one made for you a while back but never got around to giving it to you. I figured this was a good time."

Her mind slipped back to all those years ago, and she could see the hurt teenager whose father had run out on him. The concho was a reminder of both the pain from that loss and the family that Boone Ryland had made.

"Thank you," she managed to say despite the massive lump in her throat.

"I always thought you should have one,"

Dade added. "And if you decide to throw it in the creek, put a bullet in it or drape it around a picture frame, it's your right." He stooped down so he was eye level with her, and he caught on to her shoulders. "Eve, you're a Ryland, and you belong with Grayson."

The tears threatened again, and she hoped that Dade thought the cold wind was responsible. "I can't have Grayson," she said. She put the concho on her lap so her hands would be free to wheel the chair to the taxi door.

But Dade took over. "Because Grayson's too stubborn and proud."

"No. Because he's Grayson." She managed a smile when Dade helped her into the back of the taxi. She made sure she had hold of the concho, and then closed her hand around it.

Dade brushed a kiss on her forehead. "I can't do anything to change your mind?"

She didn't even have to think about this. "No."

Eve had seen Grayson's reaction the night before. He felt guilty for her injury and guilty that the bullet had almost certainly cost her a baby. That guilt would eat away at him, and he would come to her and try to make things right.

Eventually, they'd land in bed again.

And eventually the old feelings and wounds

would resurface, and Grayson would resent her for forcing a relationship on him that he didn't want.

"I can tolerate a lot of things in life," she whispered to Dade. "But I refuse to be the person who brings Grayson Ryland to his knees. I love him too much for that."

Thankfully, Dade didn't argue. He didn't question her or her logic. He simply smiled, shut the taxi door and waved goodbye.

Eve pressed her hand and the concho to her heart, hoping it would ease the pain. But that was asking a lot from a little piece of silver, even if this piece of silver was one of the most precious gifts she'd ever received. She definitely wouldn't throw it in the creek or put a bullet in it. She would keep it close to her heart.

Eve waited until the driver was out of the parking lot before she broke down and cried.

Chapter 20

Grayson cursed. He'd actually punched a singing Christmas tree and rammed it into the trash can.

He'd thought it was a reasonable reaction at the time. The tree was stupid, sitting on the dispatcher's desk at the sheriff's office and bursting into that same tinny "Jingle Bell" tune every time anyone walked past it. Well, Grayson was tired of it. Plus, it was nearly two weeks past Christmas, and if he'd had any holiday spirit, it was long gone.

Still, he'd punched a Christmas tree.

And that's when he knew this had to end.

His mood was well past the surly stage, and even the usually even-tempered Nate had demanded that Grayson *do something*. Grayson hadn't needed to figure out what his brother meant. He knew.

He had to see Eve.

So he'd forced himself into his new truck and started driving.

However, now that he was parked in front of her condo in San Antonio, Grayson was rethinking his impulsiveness. He probably should have called or emailed first. Heck, he darn sure should have sorted out his feelings and what he wanted to say to her.

What if she told him to take a hike?

That wasn't the only worry on his mind. Still, he had to see for himself that she was okay, that she had recovered both physically and mentally from the shooting.

He was about to get out of his truck, when the front door to her condo opened, and Eve backed out. She had on jeans, a dark red sweater top, and she was dragging something.

A Christmas tree.

Not a fake singing one but a real one with dry, browning branches. No ornaments, but there were a few strands of silver tinsel that caught the cold January wind and the afternoon sun. Since she was struggling with it and since he was pretty sure she shouldn't be twisting and turning her body like that, Grayson hurried over to help her.

She must have heard his footsteps because she let go of the tree and whirled around as if she'd expected to be attacked.

Hell.

She'd been having those nightmares about the shooting.

But her expression quickly went from alarm to a smile. Not the weak half-assed smile that she'd given him in the hospital. This was a real one. An Eve smile that lit up her whole face. That smile caused him to freeze.

Oh, man. She was beautiful. Always had been, always would be. And he would always feel as if it he'd been sucker-punched when he saw her.

"Grayson," she said on a rise of breath.

"Eve." His voice didn't sound any steadier than hers.

They stood there, staring, waiting. And because Grayson had to have something to do with his hands, he grabbed the trunk of the dead tree.

"Where do you want this to go?" he asked.

She motioned toward the Dumpster at the end of the parking lot where there were several other discarded Christmas trees. "The recycling truck is supposed to pick them up today," she let him know.

Grayson headed in that direction, and Eve followed along beside him. He looked for any signs of pain or limited movement, but there weren't any.

"I'm okay," she assured him as if reading his mind. "I had my post-op check up last week, and the doctor said I was healing nicely."

"Good." He cursed himself when he repeated it.

Grayson didn't hurry because he didn't want Eve to hurry to keep up with him, but he didn't dawdle, either. It was cold and blustery, and despite her *healing nicely* remark, he didn't want her outside any longer than necessary— especially since she wasn't wearing a coat. He tossed the tree next to the others and headed back.

"Would you like to come in?" she asked. The invitation was tentative, like her body language. She wasn't fidgeting exactly, but it was close.

"Yeah. I'd like to talk." And say what exactly, Grayson didn't know.

Well, except for asking her the results of the pregnancy test she'd taken. Of course, if by some miracle that result had been positive, she would have already told him.

Maybe.

And Grayson had to accept that maybe she had already written him out of her life. It seemed that way in the hospital.

Eve walked into the condo ahead of him and shut the door once he was inside, but didn't sit. She stuffed her hands into the back pockets of her jeans, causing her sweater to tighten across her breasts.

Something he shouldn't have noticed.

However, he also noticed her necklace. Not an ordinary one. It was a familiar concho with the double *R* brand of his family's ranch.

"Dade gave it to me for Christmas," she said, following his gaze. "He had it made years ago."

Funny, his brother hadn't mentioned a thing about seeing Eve or giving her a Christmas present. After Eve had left the goodbye note at the hospital, Grayson had thought all the Rylands had respected her wishes to be left alone.

Apparently not.

And he would take that up with Dade when he got home.

"The concho doesn't have bad memories for me like it does for you and your brothers," Eve explained. She shifted her weight, glanced away. "When I see it, I don't think of your father leaving. I think of all the memories of when he was there. When things were good."

Leave it to Eve to find the silver lining.

Grayson reached out and slid his fingers beneath the concho pendant. But it wasn't just the pendant he touched. His knuckles brushed against her breasts. She made a slight shivering sound and stepped back. Grayson let go of the concho and stepped back, too.

"Sorry," she mumbled. But then her chin came up. "I guess it's stupid to apologize for an involuntary response. I'm always going to feel an attraction for you, Grayson, and saying I'm sorry won't make it go away."

No. But admitting the attraction only reminded him that he felt the same about her. Not that he needed a reminder. Just seeing her had the heat sliding through him.

"Always?" he questioned. Oh, yeah. This was playing with fire all right.

She met his gaze head-on. "Always."

Their gazes held, and so many things passed between them. Questions. But very few answers, only the obvious one about this simmering heat. Yes, it would always be there.

"How are you, really?" he asked.

The corner of her mouth lifted. "Well, I'm not in any shape to haul you off to my bed, but I'm healing."

That didn't cool him down. Oh, man. He was stupid to keep at this, but Grayson had no choice. He needed to get to the bottom of this once and for all.

"Do you want to haul me off to your bed?" he asked.

He didn't quite get the reaction he'd hoped for. Eve huffed, and her hands came out of her pockets and went on her hips. "Yes. Happy now?" She didn't wait for his answer. Not that he had one. "What's this visit really about?"

He didn't have an answer for that, either. But he knew he sure as hell needed one. Grayson couldn't go back to kicking Christmas trees or to his nonstop surly mood. He had to resolve this situation once and for all.

"Well?" she prompted. She wasn't tapping her foot, but it was close.

Grayson tried to wrap his mind around his feelings, but Eve huffed again.

"I'm in love with you," she tossed out there like profanity. "I've tried not to be, but I can't make my feelings go away. So, there! Learn to deal with it." Another huff. "Would you like to know what I've been dreaming about for the past two weeks?"

Not the shooting. Grayson prayed it wasn't that.

"About *you,*" she tossed out, as well.

Grayson was relieved. Sort of. "I've dreamed about you, too."

He had to gather his breath because he knew these next few minutes would be the most important of his life. Everything was about to change.

And it all hinged on Eve.

"I'm in love with you, too." He said the words fast, like pulling off a bandage, and he was surprised that it hadn't hurt one bit. Just the opposite.

Grayson felt relieved.

That relief didn't extend to Eve, however. Her eyes widened. Her mouth dropped open. "When did you realize that?" she asked.

"A long time ago. It just took me a while to get around to saying it." And because it'd taken him too long, he decided to repeat it. "I love you, Eve."

She didn't say a word. She just stood there, mouth open, and then the tears sprang to her eyes. Grayson moved first, but she was faster. Eve launched herself into his arms.

He took things from there.

Grayson kissed her, and for the first time in his life, he didn't hold anything back. He loved her, and he wanted her to know that. He must have succeeded because the kiss quickly turned fiery hot.

Eve coiled her arms around him, pulling him closer, but Grayson kept things gentle. Or at least he tried. Hard to stay gentle with the kiss going French and with Eve pressed against him. It wasn't easy, but Grayson pulled back to remind her of her injury.

"You're not in any condition for sex," he reminded her.

"Maybe not our normal version of sex." She put her mouth right against his ear because she was obviously a twisted woman who knew that would torture him in the best kind of way.

Grayson groaned and gladly gave in to the torture. He lifted his hands in surrender while she went after his neck.

Oh, yeah.

Eve knew every inch of his body, and within seconds had him rethinking that no-sex-right-now rule.

She pulled back slightly, met his gaze and gave him a nudge with her body that had his eyes crossing. "But remember, I'm in love with you," Eve confessed, "and we can find a way to make this happen."

He froze. And Eve noticed. She went stiff, too, and some panic raced through those jeweled blue eyes. "I was talking about sex when I said we can find a way."

"Were you?" he challenged.

More panic. She stepped back, as she'd always done in the past because she didn't want to put him in a corner. Well, Grayson was sure of two things—he was crazy in love with Eve, and he wanted to be in that *corner.*

He caught on to the silver concho pendant again, and because he wanted to hear that little shiver of arousal, he let his fingers trail over her right nipple.

He smiled when he heard the sound.

And then Grayson let go of the pendant and dropped to his knees.

Eve's sexy shiver turned to a gasp. "What are you doing?"

Grayson didn't even have to think about this. "I'm asking you to marry me."

The room was suddenly way too quiet. No more shivery sounds. No gasps. Eve just stared at him, and for one horrifying moment, he thought she would turn him down.

She certainly didn't say yes.

"Why are you asking me now?" she wanted to know.

Grayson had to release the breath he was holding so he could speak. "Uh, is that a trick question?"

"No." Eve was quick with that assurance but not with the answer to his proposal.

He shrugged. "I thought it was obvious. I'm

asking because I love you. Because you're already part of the family, but I wanted to make it official. And because I want you in my bed every night."

She stared at him, as if waiting for more.

What?

That wasn't enough?

Grayson eased her down to her knees so they were face-to-face and so he could kiss her. She apparently needed a reminder of that love she'd professed for him just minutes earlier.

The kiss was long, satisfying and left them both breathless. "Say yes," he insisted.

But she didn't. She pulled back again. "Is this about the attempt to get me pregnant?"

"No." And he hoped she could see that was the honest to goodness truth. "This is about being in love with you. We can discuss the details of our future later, but for now I need an answer, and I need that answer to be yes. Because I can't imagine living the rest of my life without you."

Now, she made a sound. No shiver, but a melting sigh, and her smile returned. Eve slid her arms around him.

"Yes," she finally said. "Because I can't imagine living without you, either."

Grayson wasn't sure which he felt first—relief or happiness, but it was the happiness that filled every part of him.

Eve had said yes!

He wanted to whoop for joy and celebrate, but first he needed another kiss. Their mouths met, barely a touch at first, but in their case familiarity bred lust because this kiss quickly turned scalding hot.

Grayson wanted to tell his brothers about the engagement, but after a few more of those kisses, he knew his brothers would have to wait. Right now, he wanted to make love—gently—to his fiancée.

He got up, scooped Eve into his arms and headed for her bedroom. The kisses didn't stop. In fact, they got more heated as Eve pressed her mouth to his chin and then his throat.

"Wait!" she said the moment he eased her onto the bed.

Hell. That wasn't a word he wanted to hear. "You can't take back your yes," he let her know. "You're marrying me." And he hoped she didn't argue.

"I didn't mean wait about that. Of course I want to marry you. I've wanted that since I was sixteen."

And that made Grayson smile.

He eased them onto the bed and then rolled

her on top of him. "Then why did you say wait?" But his gaze dropped to her side. "Oh. Second thoughts about sex?"

"No." She made it sound as if he'd lost his mind. "I want sex. Trust me, I really want to have sex with you. But I have to tell you something first."

Her smile faded until she looked anything but happy.

Grayson froze again. In fact, he was reasonably sure that every muscle in his body locked up so he couldn't move. "What's wrong?"

"Uh…" And a moment later, she repeated it. She also licked her lips and bunched up her forehead. "The test was, well, it was positive."

It took a few seconds for that to sink in through the worry and the haze in his mind. "You're pregnant?" And that was something he thought he'd *never* hear himself ask Eve.

She nodded. Swallowed hard.

Eve eyed him as if he were a stick of dynamite about to go off. "I should have told you the minute you got on your knees, but I was so surprised. And happy. The only thing I could think of was saying yes. I didn't think that this baby could change everything."

He caught on to her arm. "Wait a minute." The thoughts and words were flying at him so fast that it took Grayson a moment to speak.

"You think a baby could change the way I feel about you?"

She blinked back tears. "Does it?"

Oh, man. He had some explaining to do. Grayson decided to start that explanation with a kiss. He gently pulled her down to him and did just that.

"Yes, it changes how I feel about you," he admitted. He slid his hand over her stomach. "It makes me love you even more."

Her breath swooshed out and she snapped him to her. Probably too hard. But Grayson couldn't make himself let go of her.

"But this messes up the plans you had for your life," she reminded him.

"Screw the plans." In fact, he was looking forward to a little chaos, especially the kind of chaotic love that a wife and a child would give him. He hadn't realized until now that having Eve and this child gave him something he'd never had—completion.

His life would be complete with them.

He wouldn't just have brothers. Wouldn't just be part of the Rylands. He would have his *own* family.

"So you're happy?" she asked.

Grayson wanted no room for doubt. "I'm the happiest man on earth." And he pulled her into his arms so he could hold her and kiss her.

He could have sworn he felt everything in the universe go into some kind of perfect cosmic alignment.

Or maybe that was just his heart.

Either way, this was right. No, it was better than that.

It was perfect.

And Grayson wanted to hold on to Eve and his baby like this forever.

* * * * *